MW00955105

Until the Names Grow Blurred

E. Hank Buchmann

Until the Names Grow Blurred is a work of fiction. Names, characters, places, and incidents either are the product of the author's imagination or are used fictitiously, and any resemblance to actual persons, with the noted exception of Wilfred Owen, living or dead, business establishments, events, or locales is entirely coincidental. Although Wilfred Owen is an actual person, the conversations created here are fictional and based only loosely on actual events.

Copyright © 2014 by E. Hank Buchmann
Cover Design by Rachel Oline Boruff
RachelThorntonPhotography.com

First Edition
All rights reserved under International
and Pan American Copyright Conventions.

No part of this book may be reproduced, stored in a retrieval system, or transmitted in any form or by any means, electronic or mechanical, including photocopying, recording, or otherwise—except for the use of brief quotations in critical articles or book reviews—without the expressed written permission of E. Hank Buchmann.

This book is dedicated
to my father, Edward H. Buchmann
and to the memory of my grandfather,
John E. Ottmar, old soldiers both.

EDMUND DROPPED DOWN into broken time, into the strange parade of memories. He was old now, on the way to the end, and he wanted to get it right before he forgot. Before everything faded.

Fog floats in ethereal drifts above the mired land. Rusted circles of wire, looping like dewy cobwebs, give a dull sparkle to the early morning twilight. Across the scars and wounds of this terrain, the heads of two helmeted men bob like pond turtles at play. One is holding a cigarette cupped in his hand, the other laughing at something the smoker has said. *Eine Frau, ha ha.* His head comes back, and the white of his neck shows pale against the shadows. The bullet comes before the sound and then the red flower of blood. The laugh catches in his opened throat, his teeth exiting through the back of his head.

Outside his window, in the spring dusk, the faint tingle of a chime sounded. No doubt it was louder than what he was able to hear, for he was old and his hearing had fallen away long ago. Still, the sound was there, and as he strained to listen, it drew him across a ghastly plane of time, across the mocking burden that the years had not satisfied in silencing. Even the sea waves, crashing as they did, could not proscribe this music, nor could the waves subdue his thoughts. In fact, the waves now did the opposite of what he'd hoped they'd do when he committed himself to living here. There had been no great sea in the place he longed to escape. Only a flat wasteland of mud and flooded shell craters, a mad wilderness of destroyed trees and villages, dying horses and dying men. But the ocean, with its waves plying up their strength to slam the shore, now seemed to him a watery remembrance of climbing the precipice and going over the top.

He threw off his blankets and gingerly swung his legs down from the bed. Groping for his cane, he scooted blindly through the darkened room to the window. With one hand, he reached up and drew back the curtain, exposing the room to the rising moon and the first faint shimmer of stars. The chiming was louder now, and he pressed his feverish forehead against the window, trying to see down the side of the building to find the source of the jingling noise. This was fruitless, he knew.

As he felt the coolness of the pane against his face, he heard Collins once again coming toward him across the trench, the sucking of his boots in the mud making a sound like barking dogs at his heels. *Looky what I got 'ere for you, Edmund. Bought it offa Tippon, I did.* Collins held up the bell and gave it a wiggle, causing it to jingle. *'ow's that for music, 'eh, sir?*

The night crept in more deeply, the low grinding of sadness nestling in his dreams. It was possible, in his old age, for his dreams to center on a solitary thing, something as inconsequential as a raindrop splashing a coin-size circle on muddy water. An entire dream may consist of nothing but brown mud and gray rain. But beneath these were the voices of the dead. They had never left him. He tried to write about it once, but the words did not come. They were never magical words. Not like Owen's. Never like Owen's.

The whole exercise only made it worse. So for two years after the war, he labored as a machinist's assistant, running a lathe in Pittsburgh. One day another man in the shop lost his grip on a slab of metal he'd been holding to a grinder, and the piece, hot and jagged as shrapnel, flew across the room, striking Edmund under his chin. He bled like a slaughtered hog, but the blood was not why he quit that very day. He quit because he had spent four years dodging these same kinds of projectiles, and he wanted no part of it ever again. He took a job as a night watchman so he could attend classes during the day at the city college. After three years, he emerged as a teacher. His chin still bore the scar, but that was not his only scar.

It was a long run backward every night to the cold angry town of Bullfork, Minnesota.

"Are you sunning yourself, Mr. Ellicott?"

From the chair by the lobby window where he'd been dozing, Edmund Ellicott opened his eyes and looked into the face of Brooke, the facility's activities director. A pretty creature, Brooke, laid her best smile on him, but got only a flutter of startled eyelashes for a reply. She studied the patch of sunlight that left a square of yellow on his blue trousers, touched his shoulder faintly, and then moved on toward the dining hall.

Edmund's head tipped down again, and he returned to the kitchen where he and Delores had been talking.

"They moved you out of history? Why?"

Edmund sat silently. He knew it was best to let his Aunt Delores have her full say before trying to interrupt.

"But you love history. Wasn't that the whole point of you going to school? So you could teach history?" These were not necessarily questions Delores expected Edmund to answer. "You sat right there at this very table and said, 'I'd like to pass something on.' 'That would be history,' you said. 'Because,' you said, 'I am now part of history.' And you felt it might help you too. Help you, you know, talk about it. By teaching it."

Edmund touched the sugar jar that was in the center of the table and turned it slowly as if winding an old delicate clock.

"So now what have they done?" Delores ranted.

"They need someone to do English." His voice was as steady as a train.

"English," she snorted. "You were schooled to teach history." Her fists were resting on her hips now, and she looked at Edmund

3

with enough agitation on her face to insinuate that some of this might have been his own fault. "I suppose you didn't say a word. You just took it like—"

"I studied English in college too," he said, cutting her off. He was thirty years old, but in her presence, he was still twelve. It had always been that way. "I signed a contract to teach. It didn't say what."

"Well, that's a fine thing. You should have stayed—"

Edmund stopped her again. "No! I should *not* have stayed in Pittsburgh. I should not have done anything differently. I'll teach English." He finally looked her in the face. "Have you forgotten what I've been through?"

Aunt Delores was silenced by the tremor in his words. She lifted the tails of her apron and wiped her hands, although she had only just put the apron on and her hands were clean. She saw him looking down at the tabletop again and watched him doodle idly with the sugar jar. "When do you start?" she asked.

He tried to remember now, counting backward. It had to have been 1927. It lasted two years. But when the principal finally offered to move him back into history, Edmund declined. *I'll stay in English.*

After supper Edmund Ellicott toddled back to his room and watched through the picture window the blue-gray waves pummeling the rocky shore. But he saw beyond this, and after awhile, he was seven years old again, curled inside the cocoon of a woolen blanket, lying in the back of his uncle's wagon. Even beyond the stale matty smell of the old blanket was the awful and acrid reek of smoke. Edmund needed not lift his head and look to see the savage flames or the tumbling crash and pop of devoured timber—he could hear it. He could feel it through his skin.

Here was his first taste of God in His fury.

"I think most of you know me. I'm Brooke, your activities director."

It was nice how she said *your* activities director.

"But some of you are new arrivals, so I'm going to pretend that this is the first time we've met. Now Karl here has heard me say that so many times he's probably tired of it, right, Karl?"

Karl, with his swampy, tired eyes, blinked at her.

"Before we get started with Bingo, I have a surprise for you all. Starting next week, Pillar Point Village will be entertaining some special guests. I have made arrangements with the local high school—with Mr. Gallagher—and have invited some of his students to join us for lunch. Then, after lunch, these students will partner up with some of you. It is their desire to interview you. Doesn't that sound exciting?"

Brooke paused for affect. Let it sink in. Some of the residents looked unfazed, as if they hadn't even heard her. Others seemed bothered. They didn't always like strangers. Especially young strangers. It had been too long ago since they had been young. The whole thing would make them feel uneasy. But Brooke knew all that.

"Don't worry," she went on. "We won't rush this. We want you to become friends first."

Edmund hated it when people said things like that, things like *friends*, as if she actually expected some teenage kid to give a rat's ass about them. Who was she fooling? Besides herself. He tried to picture this. *Hey, who's the old man? Oh. This is my new best friend, Edmund. He's telling me his life story.* Sure, sonny.

Across the room, a man raised his hand. A new guy Edmund hadn't seen before. Tall. His hair, like everybody else's, was chalk-white, but most of it, cut short, still covered his head. Edmund thought he looked like a horse with his long face. When he spoke, Edmund saw his great corn-kernel teeth, like a horse's. But there

5

was something else, something unsettling about the scowling eyes. Or was it something *around* the scowling eyes.

"Yes, Gus. What is it?" Brooke turned her whole body toward Horseface.

"Ve don't have to do diss, do ve?"

"No, Gus. You don't *have* to. But it would be nice if you participated."

What's this? Edmund thought. Another dissenter.

All through Bingo he studied this new fellow over the top of his glasses. Horseface. And when the game was over and they dispersed to their beds for an afternoon nap—which is what their lives had been reduced to—he saw that Gus walked B Hall to the very end. That put him in direct line with Edmund's own room. Edmund wondered, as he stretched on his bed, if this Horseface was the one with the chime.

Later, in the pitch of darkness, he thought about his friends. His real friends. They were all dead, of course. He had no one left. Even his lovers were ashes now too. Then he thought of Brooke and he frowned. What would a sixteen-year-old kid ever understand about what he had to say?

Before sleeping, he thought about the father he did not remember. Edmund was only two when his father was struck in the middle by a cannon ball while charging up San Juan Hill. Things were getting mixed up for him now. He was starting to think that maybe he *did* remember his father. His father's voice. His touch.

No, he was just mixed up.

But not about all of it. He was *not* mixed up about all of it.

6

The scar that was Bullfork cut against the frozen base of the mountain called Benedict Bluff. Nobody knew, or cared, why it was called that, only that Bullfork had its face to Minnesota and its back to Canada. It was an Indian town, rough as a saw blade and prosperous as a flattened penny. The chief occupations were vagrancy and disorderly conduct, with an occasional stretch working in the mills. No longer able to keep their rented house, the recently widowed Agnes Ellicot and her young son, Edmund, found refuge living with Agnes' sister, Delores, and her husband, Uncle Victor. Their name was Suskin, and they owned Suskin Mercantile in the middle of the only street in Bullfork.

These years came with the haze of childhood, the routine of rising and eating and play. Nothing actually held together in the pool of memory until Edmund was five. Here came the realization that when Agnes, his mother, was gone during the days for long hours, she was, in fact, working inside Suskin Mercantile in order to help defer the added hardship of Uncle Victor feeding and lodging two more people. It was also the year that Aunt Delores became pregnant. There grew, in direct harmony with her belly, his own curiosity about what was happening. It seemed to him, at first, that she was just eating too much, but as the talk around the dinner table became more relaxed in his presence, he became more aware that a visitor of some sort was about to join the household.

It never happened. Aunt Delores suffered a midterm miscarriage, and the trauma of that served only to add to the unusualness of the year. The next year he was put in the Bullfork school—a room in the basement of the Lutheran church—where his slow and dissatisfying education was launched. What he had not known—indeed had never even realized—was that he had already been learning at home. For the greater part of his fourth and fifth years, his Aunt Delores—*not* his mother—had been patiently reading him the stories of Rudyard Kipling. These were adventures that he understood; certainly boys being raised by animals in the jungle was not so out of the ordinary for his way of thinking. After the miscarriage, when it might have seemed natural to stop such activities, she instead buried her sorrows in books. The readings became frightening stories by Hawthorne, and the man with the big forehead and little mustache, Poe—all these too frightening for him, yet he clung like a drowning boy to every delightful word. Aunt Delores' voice was like an ointment to all things bewildering. Then when he was in school and the teacher would read a childish story of two children walking to the store kicking stones, and the kicking of the stones was the most thrilling part of the tale, Edmund found himself longing for something meatier. Not something cleverly disguised to teach students their vowels.

This pattern seemed to continue uninterrupted until he was seven. By this time Edmund's mother had been seeing an Indian named Pete Lodge fairly regularly. Pete was not handsome or noble, but he always seemed to be smiling, and it was this levity that drew Agnes to him.

Edmund's father had been dead now for five years, buried somewhere in Cuba, in pieces. The cannonball that cut him in two had shortened his height by eight inches, so if they had sown him back together again, he would have barely reached five foot one. This Edmund overheard two men discussing at the Mercantile. He listened like a thief to their words, not realizing until the story was done that they had been talking about his father. How could they know all that, he wondered, unless they were there and had seen it? In fact, they had *not* been there, so Edmund, even in his green years, was able to store this information away into his child's brain, realizing that there would always be those who claimed to know more than they really did. It would be only eleven more years before Lieutenant Edmund Ellicott would remember all this, drawing back on the foolish old men whose wars were long over, if they ever had any at all, and would certainly not claim anything matching the horrors of the trenches that he himself was about to endure.

"I would like it, Edmund, if you would join us."

It was Brooke and her tiresome persistence grated on him. He had told her twice already that he did not want to be "partnered up" with any school kids.

He drew her close and said, "It's not the kids I object to. I just don't want to share my life with them." What he really meant was he didn't want to scare the living hell out of them. They were far too tender to know what he knew as truth.

Brooke and Edmund sat down together in the dining hall and scanned the group of timid high schoolers. There were a dozen of them, and they stood in awkward bunches, unsure of what to do next. It seemed that they too had been thrust into this unfortunate gala the same as the old folks had, but probably a passable grade in history or social studies hung in the balance. Finally, a fat boy with a ball cap managed to pull a smile from old Karl, and Karl patted the tabletop, directing the kid to sit down. Beatrice Ross, in her red dress and dancing shoes, drew the attention of a girl who also wore a red dress. From where Edmund and Brooke sat, they saw how the old woman and the girl contrived the fable of a bond and so sat down together. Lunch was over, but ice cream was being passed around.

Horseface was not in attendance. Edmund had looked for him but never really expected him to show. Edmund wanted the ice cream, but he didn't want to be a part of this other nonsense.

His mother was a stranger to him. He had always accepted this since it was all he could remember their relationship ever having been. Agnes always seemed impatient with the boy, where Aunt Delores was just the opposite, coddling him with her stories or with the corner piece of the cake, the piece with the most frosting. Aunt Delores always knew when Edmund was in the room; his mother never seemed to notice. But this time it was his mother's turn to get pregnant, and in any place other than Bullfork, it would have meant a scandal, but here, in this town of absent morals, it was simply life as usual. But a cloud grew over Uncle Victor because of this, and it became clear over the supper table that Pete Lodge was not father material.

In the end, it didn't matter.

Brooke had left his side and was now helping in her syrupy manner to match people up. Edmund watched this with mild interest, the way she would breeze into their midst, touch a shoulder or forearm, produce a false laugh and miraculously establish a connection between them. None of these kids seemed to have a stitch of understanding about what they were letting themselves in for.

Beatrice would bore them stupid with her stories of high society in Baltimore, dancing with Arthur Murray. Vinny would talk about his days playing saxophone in the bistros of Philadelphia, the taste of chicken and burgundy on his breath; and Karl, if he could remember his own name, might confuse these kids for his sons or daughters.

Secretly, Edmund wondered what Gus' life story might sound like. It was doubtful that any of these fresh kids would feel comfortable sitting under his dark gaze. But there was more than the crease of his unsmiling mouth to fend them off; there was another crease too. Edmund had seen it at lunch the day before, a line of welted skin, like the puckered bead made by an arc welder, only of flesh not metal. This crease started at the corner of his right eye and followed a jagged path to his ear. The eye did seem somewhat damaged, hiding itself in the depths of his dark feathered brows and piercing black pupils.

After awhile, he was relieved to see that most of the kids had been matched up. This set him on the slow march to the dessert table, his cane marking the route. With his free hand, he balanced a bowl of strawberry ice cream, a spoon already standing erect in its middle, and moved without fanfare back to his remote table.

For a long while, he worked at the cold ice cream, dragging the frosty spoon across his tongue with every bite. He was thinking about Owen when he felt someone standing behind him. Edmund's back tightened, but did not turn around. He was afraid it was Brooke again, wanting to prod him into being sociable. Sociability was not on his list today.

When he finished, he put the spoon back in the bowl and shoved the bowl to the middle of the table. Nap time, he thought. But when he rose from his chair and turned, gripping his cane, he saw her sitting there, notebook in hand, a quiet sparrow of a girl with straight hair the soft red called strawberry, so sleek it shined without effort. She looked at him for a second and then away.

"What do you want?" he snapped.

His bark was hoarse, and she blinked back her surprise. From the corner of his eye, he could see Brooke sizing them up. This was her doings—he knew it—so without another word or a parting glance, Edmund steered free from the chairs and started his shuffled march back to his room, leaving the girl to watch his retreat.

It was out of mercy for the poor girl, he thought. But in the darkness, with Collins there in the trench with him, he saw the girl's face again, the pallor of her complexion, turning slightly rosier at the top of her cheekbones only when he had turned to leave, a blush of something—was it embarrassment? And he saw her notebook, not a word written in it, and he remembered a girl he had taught many, many years ago who had that same fair face and hesitance of movement, and like this girl today in the dining

11

room, the girl of his past destroyed his sleep with her hurt and bewildered eyes.

Lutherans baptize infants and children, an act that drives Baptists into fits of incredulous scorn, which engineers no small amount of sniggering. *What can an infant know of Christ?* But Aunt Delores' pious rebuttal was—*If you are saying that a Lutheran baptism doesn't take, then you are willfully diminishing the power of the Holy Spirit. Shame on you.* Still, Edmund was neither babe nor adult when he was dowsed in the icy river at the age of eight, giving his soul to the Lord. She could just as well have had him baptized at the benevolent altar of the Lutheran church with water palmed up from the fount by the hand of Preacher Bordon, but Delores thought a trip to the river in public view would be a thumb in the eye of any Baptists who might be looking down their noses at the spectacle.

The ironic truth was that there weren't enough Baptists *or* Lutherans in Bullfork to announce any concern as to just how young Edmund received the sacrament of water and word. The most dedicated of all such worshipers were those who met faithfully at the Mud House for their daily ration of Blue Gill mash whisky, the specialty of the region. Here they drank regular toasts to the Lord, whom they believed fervently to be a connoisseur of the grape. Needless to say, this loyal crowd of Indians and unemployed mill workers drank an honored cup for the little fellow whose father was a dead hero of the Spanish-American War and hoped that his swim in the frozen river wouldn't kill him, too, in the weeks ahead.

But the Lord protects His own. This his aunt told him and he believed it.

Brooke looked crossly at him the next day for his snappy tongue and cold heart. She flitted her banishment of him for the greater part of the day, being careful to avoid eye contact, for fear of losing a grip on her anger. The frail little darling whom he had rejected the day before had apparently acted on her own, spying Edmund across the room and wandering, after plucking up her courage, to the table where he sat. Brooke had nothing to do with it; she'd watched it unfold before her and was stunned to see Edmund's reaction—the nasty snub and the thoughtless retreat down the hallway. *Fine,* her eyes said to him now, *it will be your own loss, you heartless ass.*

He pondered this while watching cars on the coastal highway dashing through the rain, their wipers making mad swipes at the downpour.

His carbine wrapped in oilcloth, Lieutenant Ellicott lay hidden beneath the folds of the fallen barn. Black night fell heavy on him as he unwrapped the covering from his rifle. Collins had crawled up behind him. He could feel him near his outstretched legs. They would lie like this until the first pink filament of dawn. Then, across the jelly of Flanders muck, a German would get careless.

"Edmund, are you down there?"

Aunt Delores stood at the top of the cellar stairs.

He did not answer.

"Edmund, there is no reprisal for honesty."

His eyes followed the shadows beneath the doorframe.

"There are things I would like to talk with you about, but I refuse to hobble down these stairs just to satisfy your stubbornness."

A long pause. "What things?" he echoed up.

"There are too many to list and they are not all bad."

"You mean about the eggs, don't you?" He had left them in their basket after gathering them while he took time to pet the rabbits, giving the neighbor's egg-sucking dog the chance it needed to devour the lot of them, nearly two dozen in all.

"If that is a confession, I'll count it to your favor. Is it a confession?"

A sniffle. "I guess."

"Well, then, get up here before you start growing vines like a potato."

It came only as a blur, but Lieutenant Ellicott gently pressed the trigger and felt the jolt of the stock against his shoulder, like a shudder, a punch, and the instantaneous and horrible blossom of brain, like damaged art, erupted alongside the German's temple. Collins patted his leg. *Com'on Elly, let's fly.*

He sat behind his desk and watched the girl write, the end of her pencil like the engine at the center of a wheel, twirling with the loops of her short strokes. Her face was close to the paper as she wrote, and he saw the top of her head where her hair parted and the top of her left ear, smooth and untanned. She was the last one; all the others had finished the test and were out in the hall making muffled sounds of farewell before trudging back to their farms or bent clapboard houses.

The girl was seventeen and knew no other thing but the loveless life she lived at home. Her mother was dead, her father old and past the age of humor, so she framed her only joy in being away from him, and school was her great escape. Edmund knew of her father and his dour outlook, and he pitied the girl, her name being Natalie, a name far too beautiful for the drab life she suffered.

He had assigned her a different book than the others. They were told to read *Great Expectations* and were given five weeks to complete it. But for Natalie he had chosen *Jane Eyre,* something to offer her a crumb of hope for a life hard-lived. At first, Edmund felt she might have thought it a cruel joke, relating all too well to the early trials of Jane as an orphan in the Reed household, but once she had matriculated into the company of Edward Rochester, Natalie's face brightened. Now, in her clumsy prose, she was trying to fashion her essay into something memorable.

The chimes battered his dreams.

The greater part of November brought the first storms of the season, and he slept with the rats and the lice at night while watching Brooke during the day, cranking her Bingo cage, or writing with chalk the activities for the week. The high school kids came again, but the strawberry-haired girl was not among them. He watched the kids settling in with the old folks with more ease this time, their pens swirling across pages of notes, the long ago stories in this house of the forgotten being resurrected again to new ears.

Karl jumped up once, thinking he was back on the railroad, getting tossed off the car by a Pinkerton man. Beatrice showed off her jewelry from her days of high society, going arm and arm with Navy boys from the Baltimore yards. Old silent Gus passed at a distance going from his room in Hall B to the little library by the popcorn machine. After awhile, he emerged with a book tucked under his arm and made his loose-gaited march back to his room.

Aunt Delores held his head in her lap, smoothing out the childish ruffles of his hair. She held the book with her other hand—*Captains Courageous*—her voice a priceless implement of reassurance. At the table, Uncle Victor worked by the oil lamp, scratching in his accounts book, his grand walruses covering his mouth, the tips showing the first signs of gray. The only other sound in the house was the faint jarring of love against their hearts.

There was Owen, sitting on an ammunition box under his tarp, his boots off, his dreary gray socks draped over a wire to dry. His white, fishlike feet shone like a picture of Christ's feet crucified. His pen was being put to a smudged slab of paper, and his dark face seemed shadowed by clouds. Clouds of war, they were, and Lieutenant Ellicott stood dully in the half-light waiting to be noticed. Owen crossed something off on his paper and then wrote something above this scribbled omission.

"Yes?" he said, not looking up.

Edmund remained still, momentarily mesmerized by the sinewy tough appearance of the man before him, the black hair, the mustache carved across his upper lip.

Finally. "I'm Ellicott, sir. Posted to your company."

"Canadian?"

"Actually, I'm American. But only barely."

"'How does that come about?"

"Geography, sir."

Owen looked up at last, his gray eyes soft as a collie's. He did not ask, but Edmund knew he was waiting for an explanation. The pen in Owen's hand twittered impatiently, his thin shoulders sagging.

"My uncle says that when I was born, my ass was in America and my winkie was in Canada."

"Your winkie?" A faint smile scored his face.

"My pecker, sir. It's my uncle's way, that's all."

Owen nodded, jovially now. "Winkie," he said again.

Edmund stood uncomfortably as rain started to pelt his backside.

He motioned to another crate with his pen, and Edmund sat down thankfully. Owen recapped his pen and put it lovingly in the pocket of his tunic. "Why are you here…what did you say your name was?"

"Ellicott, sir."

Owen's eyebrows deepened. "Unless you're wearing someone else's uniform, I gather we are both lieutenants. In other words, I mean, formality is not necessary."

Edmund nodded.

"So, why would a Canadian…I mean an American, in a Canadian uniform, be posted with the 2nd Manchesters? Haven't you boys enough to do in your own sector?" It only dawned on Owen just then that his visitor's carbine was wrapped in oilcloth and was being embraced between his knees like a cherished family member.

"Sniper, sir. I mean…"

Owen only nodded and then rested his elbows on the tips of his knees and lightly patted his face several times as if trying to revive himself. "The captain is down the line. He'll likely be the one to see you."

Edmund started to stand, but Owen stopped him. "Stay. He's a busy chap right now. He'll find you soon enough."

Edmund tried to turn onto his side. Sleeping on his back made him snore and that always woke him up, the eternal sputtering for breath, as if he was drowning. He pulled his legs up slowly so he could use them for leverage, and then after shifting his shoulders, he let gravity tip him onto his right side. He sighed as if having accomplished a great feat. His curtains, which he had taken to leaving drawn back now because of the chime, allowed the pointy rays of stars to dot the dark floor. There was no breeze tonight though, so the chime was silent. He had been dreaming, he was pretty sure. Thoughts of Owen still lingered.

Resting his gray head on the pillow, he could feel the loose skin on his arm sag against his cheek. All forms of manliness had left him long ago. He didn't have to touch himself to know that the muscle around his middle was gone, and he was as saggy there as the skin on a chicken. It saddened him to know this. He had been a fit man once. In the summers after the first war, after he left Pittsburgh, he used to climb Benedict Bluff on the weekends just for exercise. The town where he taught, in Smithfield, Minnesota, was bigger than Bullfork by two thousand souls, but was only a seven-mile drive away. So, for the first couple of years, he made weekly trips in to see Aunt Delores and Uncle Victor. He did this on horseback since in the late 1920s, he still could not afford an automobile on a teacher's salary. Four years later though, by the time he married, he had a Ford. *Damn. Now here's Dovey again*, he thought, *invading my thoughts*. There would be no falling back to sleep now he knew. Not with those memories. Of Dovey. And Dovey's sister, Etta.

Edmund pressed his face deeper into his pillow, hoping to smother the remnants of what they did together. What he did with them.

It was the same steamed broccoli for lunch. It smelled like dirty socks, Edmund thought. And the chicken had the texture of boiled tire tread. He sat in his chair trying to find the strength to lift his drinking glass. Why did they have to fill them so full? *Every day I spill it*. As he teetered his glass to his waiting mouth, he looked up.

Horseface.

Across the room, strode Gus, without a cane, his back proudly erect, his scar flashing a dull copper against his dark face. Edmund watched him with irritation. The sonofabitch has an accent, he thought. I heard it, and it sure as hell isn't French.

There was the captured prisoner. The night following an attack by the German line against Edmund's trench. The attack had been repelled, but during the counter-attack, a straggler had gotten lost or scared and hid himself in a shell hole. When Edmund's little band found him that night, he was without a weapon and was half covered with the liquid mud that seeped into the crater. Collins had seen some movement down there and signaled with a dry silent whistle. Edmund, Collins, and Richards approached the German from different directions and captured him without a fight. Richards had gotten to him first and held his knife to his throat, impressing him to keep his bloody mouth clamped shut.

Back in their trench, they pushed the prisoner into a muddy corner and called for Captain Everdean. When Everdean arrived, he had the major with him. Major Smyth took a fag from his pack and tossed it to the German, who promptly stabbed it into his mouth. Major Smyth nodded at Collins, who immediately fumbled for a match. The flame and smoke smelled delicious, and the German sucked it down hungrily.

The sun, damaged by thin clouds, was just then throwing an awkward glow across the battlefield, leveling a blue light onto the prisoner's face. His hands trembled with the cigarette and his eyes—a mix of fear and perhaps relief—shifted from one man to the other. Edmund moved close behind Everdean and stared over his shoulder at his captive. He was neither old nor young, possibly thirty with a mud-caked face and swarthy whiskers showing through the yellow-gray muck.

Major Smyth lowered himself onto his haunches and examined the man closely. According to the chevron on his sleeve, he was a corporal, or something equivalent. A trail of blood had dried and crusted on his neck, and when the prisoner saw the major looking at the wound, his fingers went up instinctively, dabbing at it tenderly. The cigarette was half-smoked now and Edmund wondered what was going to happen when it was finished. So far not a word had been spoken by anyone. The German was aware of this, too, and the silence started to disturb him, his hands shaking more visibly.

Finally Everdean spoke. "Did you check him for papers yet?" He looked from Edmund to Collins and then to Richards. They all three shook their heads at once. Everdean gestured with his chin for Edmund to search him.

Although he had no weapon, he did have several cartridges rolling loosely in a pocket. He had a pipe, the stem broken in two, an empty tobacco pouch, an army-issue spoon, a pair of dirty socks shoved in his pants pocket and a letter, folded and caked with the same mud that everyone's letters were caked with. Edmund handed the letter to Captain Everdean.

The prisoner seemed restless when Everdean looked inside the envelope and when a small square photograph fell out of the folds. The German tried to reach for it, but Collins stopped him. Instead, Edmund picked it up. It was dog-eared and carried the fuzzy image of a woman holding the muzzle of a horse and smiling into the camera with a flirty haughtiness. He showed it to Everdean, who glanced at it and then gestured for Edmund to give it back to the prisoner. They would keep the letter though. There were people in the rear who could read German, the same people who would be interrogating him. But the name on the envelope was clear enough—Henrik Scrupp.

Henrik Scrupp. Of all the Germans he had killed this was the first one Edmund had seen this close up—alive. The first one that wasn't aiming a carbine or bayonet point in his face. Of that kind, there had been multitudes.

He was thirty-four when he married. Dovey was ten years younger. Her family had moved to Smithfield from Buffalo, New York, and opened up a pawnshop. Dovey's father, a six-five giant with white hair, ran the shop only long enough for it to get its bearings, and then he turned it over to the care of his son, Maxwell, and to Dovey, and then he moved himself back to Buffalo.

Max Palvone was young and bright with a bent toward the darker crowd. It was rumored, after awhile, that some of his acquaintances were men who had followed him there from Buffalo—petty conmen, gamblers, and sharks of one nature or the other. They were alleged to conduct serious poker games in the back room that often ran for days on end and that great plans of empire were concocted there over whisky and women brought up from St. Paul.

To find Dovey in the middle of this strange setting gave Edmund pause. In pursuit of a better skinning knife and not wanting to pay what the old Yank Wilkins was asking at his hardware store, he wandered one day into Max and Dovey's pawnshop. The shop, not roomy in the first place, was crowded from floor to ceiling with myriad accessible cargo. He half expected this, having been in more than one of these shops in both Pittsburgh and in Europe, but what he wasn't expecting was the black haired temptress standing behind the counter looking at him with bright face and stabbing eyes.

May I help you with something?

At this juncture of his life, in his early thirties, Edmund had given up any idea of a romantic vitality catching on. He continued teaching English every day; still rode his horse back to Bullfork on weekends; still climbed the surrounding bluffs for exercise; still hunted and fished. His only real friend was Roger Bayless, a fellow teacher at the high school in Smithfield, but Roger was married, which made it difficult to keep after-hours company. Their relationship was cordial, even chummy at times, centering on books or a local hockey match, or the slow evolution of Ford's automobiles. As for topics, the war escaped mention. Just as well. For Edmund, those horrors were horrors still, and the less stirred the better.

That is why the image of Dovey Palvone standing behind the counter in the pawnshop like a museum painting struck him momentarily dumb.

The nights were always the worst. His back hurt. But pulling the cord by his bed was pointless at this barren hour. The nurse never came. So he endured. Enduring, after all, was something he'd trained himself to do. Like climbing those bluffs. It really made no sense doing it. He never thought of himself as one of those collegiate-type cliff climbers. The idea of climbing an actual mountain never entered his mind. This ritual he had in his younger days of scaling Benedict Bluffs was more of a devout mental exercise than a corporeal one. Doing it reminded him that he was a survivor. Everything about Benedict Bluffs was the extreme reverse of the Somme. If war was prayer, then Benedict Bluffs was the silent amen.

What day is it? he wondered. Or what day is it going to be when day gets here? Will day even get here? Am I even alive? Maybe I'm already dead. I just don't know it yet.

There was a vague familiarity to these thoughts. Not now when he was old. But when he was young. When he was young, he was so much nearer to being dead than here. Now.

He bent his neck toward the window, straining till it hurt, trying to see if there was any sign that day was coming, something in the black sky that erased everything. There was only the furry twinkling light of a fishing boat out on the sea, its mysterious yellow shine above the water, with the same roving pitch as the floaters in his eyes.

The first time he ever saw them—the floaters and flashers—he was in his late fifties. He thought he was seeing Christmas lights in his eyes. *No,* the doctor said. *It's common with old age.*

I'm only fifty-seven, he'd said. But the doctor was young and merely gave him a condescending grin. Well, I'm ninety-two now, you smart-ass, and you're probably fifty-seven. I hope you're enjoying your floaters.

Back when he was still teaching history, he heard accounts of some of Pershing's men chasing Poncho Villa across the sad landscape of Mexico. The stories told of the flat stovetop desert that sizzled everything that came to die. Horses and men in a land altogether unforgiving, a dozen against a dozen, shooting and riding and hiding all across the bristling land.

There was a whole searing world to fight in, and when Edmund thought about these stories, he pondered over how different it had been on the Western Front. There the fighting was cubical. They fought as if from boxes, the enemy as close as a thrown baseball in front of him. There were not miles of torrid rocks and caves, only shoulder-to-shoulder fighting in rain and mud and hailstorms of bullets. He would have given much to have a horse and an open hundred miles to ride in.

He would have liked to have saved a horse or two. Too often the nights of bombardment were filled with the screams of dying horses, screams more hideous than man's, more pitiable because they never wanted any part in that hell in the first place, didn't ask to be made cannon fodder for anybody.

His own horse, the one he had at Smithfield, and the one he rode on weekends back to Bullfork, was a blemished roan with a reluctance to speed but had a pleasant disposition that made up for its laziness. He called it D'Artignan after his favorite character in Dumas' great book. He assigned *The Three Musketeers* to his seniors to teach them the value of comradeship, and the book evolved into a favorite with the boys. Comradeship. Solidarity. It made him think of Owen. It made him think of those last days crossing the canal under heavy fire.

And now here he was, an old man. What would Owen say about old age? There was that one reference, but that came years later. After everything was over.

The strawberry girl was back. She was across the room, her back to him, the empty pages of her notebook gleaming like a slate of ivory.

He nursed his ice cream, pulling the spoon across his cold tongue. He watched her, her small shoulders covered by a white blouse, puffy delicate sleeves, her hair as glossy as a sunset. She reminded him of nobody. Not Dovey or Etta. Not even Natalie, that suffering student of so long ago. No, this girl was her own self. A rejected starling. He had hurt her and now she would not even turn his way.

Edmund pushed away his empty bowl and crossed his arms over his chest. She was trying to be brave. Oh, how many times had he seen that? All those kids—all those years. For a moment, he saw Natalie's papers before him, her clipped cursive stroke in black deliberate ink marks, her valiant efforts. He remembered reading it, and even at this very instant, sitting in the dining room, remembering, he could see again his own pen making a mark in red at the top of her paper—*A.*

It was not a gift. She had earned it.

He felt suddenly on the verge of tears. Knowing all that came later in that poor girl's life. That bastard Hemmings.

Edmund uncrossed his arms and placed his hands over his face as if to block out all this sadness. He felt Brooke brush by him, wordlessly, a rush of air, the scent of her perfume. Staring into the darkness of his palms, he saw the only road left to take. It was the same as finding his way back to the lines during a night patrol, the blackness of inner instinct, knowing the right way to turn.

After uncovering his face, he waited for Brooke to pass again, but she made no such move. He was an outcast to her now. So taking a grip on his cane and pushing himself up against the tabletop he rose to his feet, jockeying them so that they both faced in the same direction. Then he shuffled like an injured crane across the room, weaving invisibly through the maze of tables and chairs and humanity, young and old, until he stood feebly at the back of the strawberry girl. He was startled for a moment at the decrepit sight of his own wrinkled hand as he reached out and touched her shoulder.

The gunmetal was cold against his chin.

How long had he been lying there? A prism of rosy luminosity had formed on the bowl of the scope, but the cross hairs remained vivid. Against the vexing first light of dawn, he detected the black outline of a helmet. He did not wait. He had waited long enough. The rifle's bark. The punch against his shoulder—across the mudfield, the last thing he saw was the helmet explode and fly like a clipped raven into the air, the German's head torn in two.

"I need a knife," he said. "A skinning knife. Do you have skinning knives?"

The black-haired young woman tilted her head for effect and smiled. "Right over here, in the case."

Edmund followed her to the display case, watching her long legs deliver smooth gliding steps across the plank floor, as if her feet were on rollers, her poise erect with self-confidence. She brushed the glass with an open palm and then looked up and smiled, her teeth shockingly white against her black hair. There was a lightness in her expression as if she had been expecting him, as if she knew him and had not seen him for a while.

He forced himself to look into the display case, but for a moment, he had forgotten what he was there to find. There were knives of every sort and pistols and black leather clubs like those used in the big cities filled with crime. He'd read about such things in detective magazines or in stories by O. Henry and Chandler. And there were skinning knives, too, just as she'd said.

In his winter coat, he suddenly felt very hot, so he unfastened the front buttons and pulled it open across his chest. The girl looked at him, watched every move his fingers made, as if she herself were a gambler, watching the other player's hands for a clue of what cards he might be holding. He had an urge to run, to just say goodbye and head for the door. Instead, he asked to look at a knife—*that one*, he said, pointing. She unlocked the case and drew out the knife and placed it on the glass countertop. Even lying there, motionless, the sharp blade seemed to cut the air of its own accord. He felt the bone handle, lifted it for weight, tested its balance, all the while only half comprehending what he was doing. He already knew he was going to buy it.

"How much?"

She pulled a small tag from inside the showcase, but instead of telling him the price, she simply held the tag out for him to see—$3.50, written by hand with ink. He winced. It was a lot of money for a used skinning knife, even a good one like this one. His eyes moved slowly upward from the tag, following her slender waist, the small protrusions on her sweater that were her breasts, and into her face. Looking there into her eyes was like staring down the barrel of a loaded gun. For an instant, he thought it a warning, but when she smiled, it dissolved like a scattering of birds. She laughed, open mouthed, and said she had grabbed the wrong tag. The knife was really only two dollars, not three-fifty.

He nodded. "I'll take it."

"What is your name?"

"Huh?"

She laughed again. "I need your name to put in our sales book. It's what we do. My brother is very picky about things like that."

"Edmund Ellicott."

She found a green ledger near the cash register and opened it to a page that was three-quarters filled with markings. She dipped a pen into an ink well, and he watched as she wrote down his name, her script deliberate with a lack of flair. When she finished, she asked him if he'd like a box or a bag for the knife.

He shook his head. "I'll carry it like this, thanks."

She stuck out her hand, her fingers pinched together as if cupping water. "I am Dovey Palvone," she said. "Glad to meet you, Edmund Ellicott."

He took her hand, and the skin on the inside of her wrist where his fingers reached felt like the soft insides of a lily blossom.

Life was nothing but an extended dream now—a dreamland—an awakeness fogged by memory. He remembered when he was eleven, the year the dam up at Thunder Mountain burst, flooding the valley below. He had gone with Uncle Victor on horseback up the side of the mountain to help in the rescue operation and to see how many of the people in the little village had survived. The two of them camped in the trees the first night, warmed by a fire, eating beans from a can. Victor gave him a taste of brandy from a flask to help keep him warm, and it put him to sleep there on the pine needle bed.

The next morning as they followed the escaped water into the valley, they came across an eddy that held the bodies of some who did not make it. They looked like frogs in their drowned, dead postures, legs splayed out at their sides at grotesque wishbone angles, as if demonstrating some ancient dance of the dark tribes, their bellies bloated, eyes swollen open in eternal sightlessness. The carcasses of horses floated beside them in punished death.

Edmund thought there was no sight more terrible than this. Yet in seven short years, he would witness the wholesale slaughter of great many more numbers of men, walking almost voluntarily to their deaths against a hail of machine gun bullets, as if this sort of stupid obedience would somehow bring the nations of the world to their senses.

Now, in his bed, he tried to erase these thoughts, but they were like the relentless bullets that could not stop themselves. His only recourse in those days was to fight back. But now, tonight, against the memories, there was no recourse, only surrender. These ghosts were as much a part of him as his sore feet, his weak arms, his eyes and nose, his very mind. This shell of tired bones that he had become now clung only to the past and to the impatient hope of a final peaceful dying for himself. That he had survived so much already still amazed him.

He had touched the strawberry girl's shoulder that day, and when she turned around, she blinked up at him with velvet, almost translucent eyelashes, a pale timid face and the sudden non-expectance of what might follow. From his hand, he passed to her an old silver dollar that he always carried in his pocket. Hesitantly, she received it, looked at it, saw the date—1917—and then raised her face up to him again. This time he strained an awkward smile and nodded. He gestured to her blank notebook and motioned for her to follow him, and then he turned and shuffled back to his table. She followed, self-consciously, still remembering his bad behavior of two weeks ago, fearing deception perhaps.

They sat down together, alone and away from the others, and Edmund tapped a finger at her notebook. She opened it shyly, embarrassed by its emptiness of words.

He looked at her face closely, almost too long, observing her pink skin, the kind of skin that often accompanies fearful girls with strawberry hair, as if the sun was an enemy to this fair skin and so had abandoned its duty of making it brown and healthy. She laid the coin on the table.

"I found that about ten years ago. Some drugstore clerk gave it back to me for change. I've been packing it around like a talisman since."

Her eyelashes fluttered nervously.

"Don't worry," he said. "I've come to my senses."

She braved the smallest of grins.

"I'm Edmund. Edmund the sorry old soldier. Come raging like a mad hen. I showed you my most awful self. But you haunted my sleep. That's what you did. Serves me right."

She nodded shyly. "I'm Katie," she said with a voice every bit the sparrow's.

"Are you here because you want to be? Or is it required of you?"

"I wanted to. At first."

"Until I made like an ape?"

She didn't answer, but it was obvious.

Edmund gazed at the ceiling, as if lost again for a moment. Finally, he said, "Katie, being old is more than just being old."

At that she took up her pen and wrote those words.

"There's a man in town looking for you, Edmund." It was the barber's boy, Jeff, his long pants dragging in the dirt, his straw hat dangling from a string around his neck. He was out of breath. Edmund was fourteen, three years older than Jeff, but they knew each other from school.

"Who wants me?"

"I told you—some man. He gave me two-bits to fetch you."

"What's he look like?"

"He ain't from around here. Walks with a cane though. And a hat like them army men wear."

"And he asked for me? He asked for Edmund Ellicott?"

"By name."

Edmund had been sorting cans of beans on the shelf of his uncle's store. The barbershop was all the way down on the other end of Bullfork. Aunt Delores came in when she heard Jeff's voice, swooping into their business like a curious magpie.

"What's this about a man wanting Edmund?"

Jeff repeated his story.

"I don't know any strangers," Edmund said. "I better go on down there though."

"You'll do no such thing."

"Ma'am," Jeff spoke up, "the feller gave me a twenty-five cent piece to come find Edmund. He don't look like no trouble. Just an old man."

"How old?" Delores asked.

"Old as my pa, I'd say."

Delores rolled her eyes. "Your pa isn't old. He's younger than me."

"Sorry, ma'am. I didn't—"

"You go on back and tell that man that if he wants to see Edmund, he's going to have to come up here himself. Edmund's working."

But Edmund had already taken his apron off and was taking steps toward the door.

"Where do you think you're going?"

He turned and stared at her. "Aunty, in my life I never had anybody looking for me. Not by name. I got to see what he wants."

Delores knew she had lost. For all her protective nature, Edmund was not a child anymore, and Victor had already scolded her a time or two to give the boy some growing room.

Jeff joined in again. "He's some crippled, Mrs. Suskin."

Delores crossed her arms. "I'll expect you back in fifteen minutes." It was her last grab at authority, but she said it with a simper of defeat.

Half a block from Suskin's Mercantile Jeff grabbed Edmund's shirtsleeve. "I didn't want to say nothing in front of your aunt, but the old man's got a gun."

Edmund stopped walking and stood looking at Jeff. "A gun?"

"A rifle. He was sittin on the bench outside of the jail office. Right there. Had the rifle standing straight up, right between his legs. Looked like he was waitin for the next war."

Edmund gaped at Jeff. "Where was Sheriff Ben?"

"Sittin right there with him."

The boys turned together and continued their march, a bit faster now, in the direction of the jail office.

Edmund woke thinking someone was in bed with him. In his sleep, his extra pillow had been shoved down against his back and it felt like another warm body beside him. The nurse had given him a pill for a backache after supper, and now in the middle of the night, he felt lightheaded and disoriented. *Is that you, Dovey?* There was only silence. She must be sleeping. He lay still, not wanting to wake her.

They had fallen asleep talking in the dark bedroom. About Etta, her sister. They had both worked hard that day, he in the classroom and she in the pawnshop. It had snowed, and Edmund had helped shovel the snow from around the school. Later, when he entered the pawnshop, he was surprised that Dovey was not at the counter. Max thumbed in the direction of the backroom. When he found her there, she was sitting on a chair, face blank as a board. *Etta's husband hung himself.* She burst the words out as if practicing a poem. Four words. That night in bed, she lay motionless. But now, as he rolled over to speak to her, he found only a pillow, the reflection of the open curtains in the mirror, and he remembered that he was old. Outside the chime jingled faintly in the night.

Owen was trying to bring an open pan of water to boil when Lieutenant Ellicott approached.

"Join me?"

He removed his helmet and ducked inside Owen's shelter.

"Fire's weak tonight. If I can get a bloody flame, we'll have

31

our tea."

Edmund sat on the same ammo box he had sat on only two nights before.

"Cap find you?"

He nodded. Owen had his helmet off, too, and Edmund studied him. Owen's dark hair was longish on top and parted severely in the middle. His mustache seemed somewhat more trimmed, and in the meager glow of the feeble fire, Owen's dark eyes seemed almost to disappear inside his head. A handsome man, Edmund thought, and a bit too civilized for a place like this.

"Tea'll be weak, too, I'm afraid. Supply's low and me mum hasn't sent the good china yet." It was a good joke, and they both laughed.

Owen gestured to Edmund's wrapped rifle. "Have you put that old girl to work yet?"

Edmund was glad for the darkness for he could feel his face flush. He was a killer among killers, and yet there was something about being a sniper that seemed remarkably more cold-blooded.

"Not yet," he said. "Too foggy."

"Do you ever—" Owen stopped, pulling the pan off the fire instead. "Here's some leaves for you. And I'll pour. Watch so I don't spill."

Edmund held out his tin cup and watched Owen, his hand slightly jittery, tip a portion of hot water into it. The black aroma lifted to their nostrils, and they both moaned with pleasure.

"To the King," Owen said, raising his cup. Then he laughed and said, "I forgot. You're American. You don't care about that bloody rubbish. You chaps had it out with the King already."

Edmund raised his cup and said, "To Kipling then?"

"Of course. Kipling. Excellent. Excellent. To Kipling."

And they drank.

He was thinking about William Faulkner. *The Sound and the Fury.* Faulkner's style of writing referred to as the "stream of consciousness," where the narration follows the wandering, oftentimes up-and-down thinking of the character. It was difficult to teach Faulkner to his students, difficult even himself to follow sometimes. And yet, here he was, Edmund Ellicott, an old man, living that very life—a stream of consciousness life— where his thoughts wandered, where his thoughts weaved and ducked, not always staying put. It was difficult now to focus.

One minute he was thinking about Dovey and the next he was in the war again. He was never far from the war, but sometimes he could still smell the smoke of the killing fire. Or the loving voice of his aunt. There was the chime, too, and the suspicions about Horseface, a carbolic burning in his throat whenever he thought about him. And that always led to Owen. Which led back to the war. Was it Caddie or was it Quentin who kept the class reading Faulkner? The whole family, ridiculous as purple asparagus. Stupid Benjy.

And that soulful expression on Natalie's face when she realized what Quentin did to himself. Or the affecting gloom of Etta. Her husband and Quentin, brothers in self-slaughter.

All this on the edge of sleep. Owen said it, or wrote it—*the steady running of the hour.* That's what life has been reduced to.

Katie's hair seemed redder today. Brighter.

"That's a nice sweater you're wearing," she said. It sounded rehearsed, as if she had been practicing a new method of engagement. Their first time actually sitting together had been forced, nervous. Her questions had been typically juvenile, typically typical. *How old are you?* Ninety-two. *Where were you born?* In the upstairs bedroom of my grandmother's house. *How many children did you have?* One. *Boy or girl?* Girl. *Where does she live?* Somewhere.

How could he tell this innocent little redheaded girl with the pink skin about his daughter? He'd have to tell her about Dovey then too. And Etta.

"Can I ask you some more questions about your daughter?"

"Why?"

"I won't if you don't want me to."

"Why do you want to?"

Their eyes met now in what seemed a minor test of wills. "Because it seems interesting to me that you don't know where she is."

"I know where she is. She is in her own place."

This answer was so ridiculous it made Katie laugh. "Mr. Ellicott, I'm already behind everybody else in this class. Thanks to you. So I'd—"

"Thanks to *me*? What's that supposed to mean?"

For the first time, she set her jaw. She blew back a fall of bangs and glared at him. "I have an idea, Mr. Ellicott. I have an idea about how I want to write this and you're not helping me."

"An idea, heh. And what kind of idea is that?"

She sat up, straightening her back, pushing her robin egg breasts against her blouse. Twisting up the corners of her mouth, she leaned close to him. "I want to ace this assignment. I want an A. And I'm not going to get an A asking you how old you are."

Edmund returned her stare glumly, and she looked momentarily unsure of herself for having spoken so boldly.

Incensed by this reaction, he spoke gruffly to her. "Don't you dare look beaten. You've made half your case. Now give me the rest."

She hesitated.

"Come on," he said. "I won't be party to a pushover." He was back in the classroom again, his ears turning hot with excitement. "What's your so-called idea?"

She swallowed and then said, "I want more. I know what Kenny has." Her eyes angled in the direction of a boy sitting with Herzog the ex-boxer. "He's sitting on a goldmine. Kenny even

34

told me so. Said Mr. Herzog is telling him about every fight he ever had. About a guy he actually killed once. In the ring."

"So?"

"So!" She sounded exasperated. "You said you were an old soldier. Why are you making this so difficult? Talk to me."

"You want me to be more interesting than Herzog over there so you can get an A?" He put his fist heavily on the table. "Look at that kid. Look at Kenny. Look at his body. He's like a melted Popsicle sitting there."

They both looked.

"Look at his face. He's not interested in getting an A. He's interested in getting a story. Kenny's already moved past the grade. He wants the experience. He wants *inside* Herzog. He doesn't care if he gets an F or an A. It's about the experience."

Katie was blindsided by this. When she looked back from Kenny, there was shame in her expression. Her head nodded as if on a string.

"You want a story, young lady? I can give you a story. But what kind of stomach have you got? This won't be about killing anybody in a boxing ring. This is about...about wholesale butchery. Are you strong enough for *that*? I don't think so."

Her bottom lip began to tremble, and at first, Edmund misjudged it as fright. But when her chin jutted out and the color rose up across her young neck, he saw instead that it was fury, plain and simple.

"I am tired of getting pushed around by you." The words crossed the space between them like an electrical arc. "You're just an old bag of noise," she hissed.

Edmund looked at her, saw an angry tear trembling at the edge of her eyelash. "You think you're ready?" He seemed to be coaxing her now. "Well, we will soon know."

She flung open her notebook stubbornly, not looking at him.

There was a disturbing knot of triumph stabbing him in the gut. I'll teach this pony something. An acid smile pricked the corners of his mouth. For a long moment, he closed his eyes.

Then he said, "Listen. For four years, I was the Angel of Death."

Old D'Artagnan. The faithful listener. Later, in a book by Steinbeck, Edmund read about the hired hand and his insistence that the boy talk to his new red pony, to give him human conversation. The horse may not understand, but conversation built companionship and trust. This came years after D'Artagnan was gone, buried like a dear friend in a corner of Uncle Victor's property, a grave dug by Edmund himself, alone in the dying light of a sad day.

But while D'Artagnan lived, Edmund had practiced this very thing. For all those early years of teaching while the horse carried him from Smithfield to Bullfork, a wide band of secrets were told. No horse west of the Mississippi—with the Mississippi being so close at hand—had heard more William Cullen Bryant recited, or untold stories of warring brutality, than good D'Artagnan. No living man or woman had ever been told about Flanders, not even Uncle Victor or Aunt Delores. Only this horse. He tried to strike a balance so as not to grieve poor D'Artagnan, thus the soothing refrains of "A Summer Ramble": *The quiet August noon has come / A slumberous silence fills the sky / The fields are still, the woods are dumb / In glassy sleep the waters lie.*

Edmund could feel the horse's muscles relax at this. After all, tales of the horrible deaths of D'Artagnan's brother-horses in the Great War were not kind anecdotes to share with your truest companion. Therefore, upon that first day of meeting Dovey Palvone in the pawnshop, the stuttering bewilderment of nonsensical love-talk filled the horse's ears. Edmund would have been embarrassed scarlet to utter these words in the presence of anyone other than D'Artagnan, but with this, his closest friend, he spilled forth.

Her eyes—the very black pearls of the Sea of Cortez. He doubted that. The Mediterranean perhaps. But this was his fantasy, so he

36

continued. The trademark olive skin of an Italian-bred daughter. Who could he think of to compare her to? He had read nothing featuring Italian heroines. Again it was only Bryant's words that came to him. *Come talk of Europe's maids with me, / Whose necks and cheeks, they tell, / outshine the beauty of the sea, / White foam and crimson shell.*

He and the horse arrived in Bullfork before any of this was settled.

Lieutenant Ellicott lay invisible beneath a fallen barn door, his scope facing away from the rising sun. He had slept in that stretched position for an hour, his body trained long ago to remain still even in unconscious sleep. There had been so many hours of hammering his body into discipline, overriding the pain of cramped muscles. Zoning it out. Effectuating a reward worth the pain. The prize of another killed German.

Even here there was too much time to think.

Over the top at Vimy Ridge. His first horrifying race across Death's field.

Up and over. One foot down, another foot down—one, two, three—counting aloud in his head for some unknown reason, seeing ahead the sudden lift of gray smoke from the machine guns and their rattling dance-tune—the solemn odd thud of bullet into body and the plopping down as if unexpectedly struck. Weary, too tired to walk another step and only the dead in the ugly noiseless death.

He saw it no other way.

Somehow his feet still moved but with no—absolutely no—recollection of his arms or of his rifle. Only his legs. He felt as if only his head and his legs floated together like a lost balloon. He heard the bees of bullets buzzing and didn't understand how he could still be afoot when all around men keep lying down like shot cattle, shot buffalo, dropping without a sound, as stupid as the dumb creatures.

Suddenly, there was the wire and the vibration of the machine guns so close and still he was not hit, and like a dream awakening, he discovered his hands and his arms and his rifle as if for the first time, and he was shooting, and he heard his mother's screams from the burning house, and he was through the wire somehow, and he had killed a man, and they were up and running, and the Germans were running, and then the earth rose up to hit him in his face, and when he tried to get up, he couldn't...his foot caught in wire and men ran over the top of him—feet on his back—and suddenly, he was up leaping across a trench still firing his rifle until after-long-after he sat on the treeless plain at the side of a man shot through the throat, and the man's only words were the gurgled resolution of his fast approaching death and the blood-spoken name of his sweetheart waiting.

Edmund shook into awareness, his heart racing.

Should he pull the cord? Was he dying?

Let it come then. After all he had been through, why should he be afraid now? Was there a reason for all this delay? Why did God spare him then—why was He sparing him now? For what?

There was a black-haired woman he wished he could hold now. Her thin-boned sweetness. Her unexpected love. Oh, to hold her again only for this night. To touch her shoulders. To kiss her neck.

In the middle of this miserable night, he began to cry. An old man sobbing into a wasteland of memory, a feeble frame trying to shake loose from his breaking heart.

"I was ten years older than her."

He had the old coin out again and scooted it across the table with his finger, a child at play.

"What did she look like?" Katie asked. She hadn't written a word yet, only listened.

"She wasn't big boned like Roselyn Russell. She was thinner. Thinner than your traditional Italian girls in those days. She wasn't Sophia Loren at all. Maybe she was only part Italian. She had the hair though. Black as a raven's wing."

"Was it love at first sight?"

"What do you know about that?"

"Nothing, personally," Katie said, feeling reproached. "But I read books. I see movies. Some people just fall over like that."

"You think so, huh?"

"I think *you* did. I think you did, and you're just not telling me."

Edmund tried to feign a blasé manner, but Katie shook her head. "You fell all over yourself, didn't you? Saw a pretty face and it was over. Lights out."

"Lights out." He repeated her words with irony and then seemed to slip unexpectedly into another dimension. Katie perceived this detachment, saw his eyes suspended like a pair of motionless orbs, and she thought she had lost him.

But through it all, his voice emerged, like a steamy breath, remote and tender. "In all the time I knew her—I never knew her. She was utterly inscrutable. When they dig up the mummified bodies of women frozen somewhere on a mountaintop, they can fill in the pieces. They can reconstruct her and say, she looked this way. Or she looked that way. This was her last meal. Or she died waiting for her rescuer. But Dovey? I knew her not. I knew not what made her rise in the morning. Or what made her lie down at night. She was as cold as a slab of granite. And as hot as a coal-fed engine. She was molten mercury in bed."

Katie did not move; nor did she blink.

"Naked, she was a deity. She liked to be touched. Liked my hands to move from her long lovely neck down across her breasts and over her hips. She would lie there as if on display. A virgin trophy for the Mayans."

Color rose in Katie's face, but she dared not speak.

"There are animals less savage than she was. A shrieking jackal, she was. Touching her was like the jungle drawing up close to the bed. She heaved and clawed like a panther. In the darkness, the moon would peek through the window like a hungry voyeur. And in that light, she glowed like a bowl of rubies. When she was like this, I disappeared. It was like I wasn't even there anymore. Her eyes would become stones then, dull and unfeeling, and I feared her. As if her desire to be devoured had passed into something else. The hot becoming the cold."

Katie's eyes were wide. Her pen had been dragging across her notebook without her knowledge; fiery notes that made the paper crackle as if aflame.

"Yes. It was *something* at first sight. Was it love? I'll never know."

He came out of the forest that was no longer a forest. It had been a great battlefield, but the battle was over, and nothing stood as it had stood before. Dusk approached and the gray sky hung without pity in the few remaining trees. The field was strewn with swirls of mud and patches of snow. Here and there bodies remained, left behind in the panic of flight. A rearguard might see him and shoot him, but he didn't care. He walked boldly amongst the wreckage of war, looking for life where life no longer existed. Only himself.

For a long time, he slogged through the muddy waste, turning dead men over with the heel of his boot. There lay at his feet a man whom he knew. Private Seymour he was, with no visible sign of blood, only the bloodless white face staring into a distant world, a world Ellicott had not yet seen but would soon. Or so he believed. *We will all die,* he thought. *Before this is over, we shall all die.* Seymour looked relieved. Not exactly peaceful, but certainly aware of what falling here in this wooded battlefield meant—that he need not fight again.

Ellicott closed Seymour's unseeing eyes and trudged on. Beyond lay a cluster of bodies. One-two-three-four-five-six. Fallen like a confusion of dominos. A direct hit from a shell. One fellow lying crosswise as if reclining on a couch. Another bent impossibly double with his head between his knees. Tunics pulled up to their necks, showing fleshy white chests and bellies. One minus a boot. Another missing an arm.

Such hideous art was impossible to look away from.

The man was still sitting in front of the jail office when Edmund and Jeff came up, trampling like a pair of colts. And just like Jeff had said, there, propped up like an ensign, was the rifle, his arms around it as if spooning a lover.

"That's him," Jeff said, elbowing Edmund.

"Step forward, lad," the sheriff ordered.

Edmund glanced at Jeff and then moved toward the plank porch.

"This here is Mr. Ripley Marshall, Edmund," Sheriff Ben said. "He's traveled a long way to see you. He needs to catch the next train. But if you let him talk with you for a spell…well, I think you'll know soon enough."

The man did not stand, but he threw down such an amazingly sociable smile, Edmund could not resist drawing closer. Mr. Ripley Marshall was in his late forties it appeared and was decked in white Panama pants and jacket. He looked as though he had just arrived from the tropics—or was going there directly. He wore canvas shoes, and one of his fingers was missing from his left hand. Upon his head was a matching Panama hat with a thin band of sweat circling the brim. His face seemed scorched by the sun, but his eyes were blue and kind and his smile remained like a neon welcome mat.

"I come to set the story right," Mr. Ripley Marshall said.
Edmund stood before him blankly.
"About your Pap."

Men do all kinds of foolish things when it comes to women.
Falling into a stupor at their feet is but one. Looking directly past
their hearts and straight into their eyes is a ruinous venture. God
Himself will tell you that the eyes are the factory of iniquity.

In the months that followed Edmund's first sighting of Dovey
Palvone, he filled his waking hours with fantastical imaginings
of her and his nights with lucid dreaming. He felt foolish in his
mid-thirties falling so stupidly for a girl as young as she. His
little one-bedroom house was a disgrace of bachelorhood and
could certainly not be of any use in luring a girl into matrimony.
Matrimony! What was he thinking? He barely knew her — in fact,
knew nothing of her. Except that she was very pretty and she
smiled often when he came into the pawnshop, and because of
his frequent visits, it became more than obvious he was trying to
woo her.

A clumsy lout. That's how he saw himself. If he had been
called on to scale a cliff, or track and shoot a moose, or better, give
an explanation of an Archibald MacLeash poem — these things he
could do. But to act like anything but an amateur in the business
of love was impossible. Love, much less marriage, had never
entered his mind.

"Are you...would you be interested in driving into Oswald
this Saturday and going to a picture show?" He was nearly
panting after such a speech.

"I've never been to Oswald. Is it far?"

"Twenty-two miles. I go there occasionally." It was a lie.

She turned her head and gazed across the room in the direction
of her brother who was rubbing a cloth across a vase to bring it
to a shine. There was a wicked intent in the way she allowed

Edmund to study her face at that angle.

"Max," she said, "might it be possible to leave the store on Saturday? Mr. Ellicott here has just asked me to the picture show in Oswald." She waited for Max's disinterested reply.

It took a minute before finally he said, without expression, "Go. I was thinking of closing early anyway."

Turning back to Edmund she beamed. "What time?"

Horseface sat sipping his apple juice, his slack lips barely touching the rim of the glass. The scar looked duller today. But the angle seemed right.

Edmund stared, his hand holding a spoonful of oatmeal halfway to his mouth. In that dim foggy bay of his mind where the war still existed, he felt again his Krag against his shoulder. In front of him they were falling. Trying to cross the canal. Trying to throw up makeshift pontoons. But they were falling. And then *Owen* fell. Turning his back to the enemy so he could direct his men, Owen fell. Hit. And Edmund, following the killing shot to the flat grass, aimed the Krag and fired. The German twisted sideways. The German machine-gunner twisted to his left, spinning in the direction of his wound.

The spoon with the oatmeal quivered in his hand, so he slowly lowered it back into the bowl.

Thoughts were getting mixed up again. He thought it was Friday, the day the kids came. The day Katie came to see him. But Brooke said it was only Thursday. How could it only be Thursday when it had already been Thursday? Was she trying to confuse him?

He thought about each day, but couldn't get past Monday. It all seemed to twist around in his head.

In the dayroom, Edmund blinked at the television. President Reagan was giving the Russians more hell. The sound was off, and he sat in a chair watching the flickering screen. An old movie would come on soon. That is if it was on the right channel. It was getting more difficult to read the numbers.

Back in his room, he decided to read. He couldn't read lying down anymore because his bifocals made the page blurry. So he had to sit at his little table and hold his big magnifying glass with one hand. That made it easier, but made it more difficult to turn the pages, holding the magnifying glass, but it made seeing the words easier. He glanced across the room and saw his book still open to the page he had been reading that morning. Thornton Wilder had just killed off one of his main characters—and the book wasn't even half over.

He concentrated. Why was it only Thursday? What had happened to the missing days?

The theater in Oswald was closed because the reels had not arrived from Minneapolis the night before, so Edmund took Dovey to a restaurant instead. He ordered a chicken fried steak and she had fish. There were green beans with bacon and mashed potatoes, and afterward they shared a bottle of wine. The wine made Dovey's face flush, and she confessed she had never tasted wine before, never drank alcohol at all before.

"I don't drink a lot of wine. Not anymore. After the war, I drank quite a bit. In France. It was good." His sentences were terse and tainted with childish insecurity. But she didn't seem to notice. She didn't talk much herself, but as the evening wore on, Edmund found that if he pretended he was talking to one of his students, a greater confidence emerged. He was, after all, something of a learned man.

"Did I hear your brother say you were from Buffalo?"

She nodded.

"I passed through Fort Niagara once after I was mustered out."

"So you saw the Falls?"

His eyes grew large. "I stood and watched that water for an hour." He shook his head. "So much power. It made me feel insignificant."

"I knew someone who killed herself, falling in the river," Dovey said suddenly.

"Really?"

"She was in love with another man. But she couldn't have him. He was a politician and already married and so—"

"That's awful."

"—so she threw herself over the falls."

He watched her mouth move as she told this story, her lips providing full expressiveness, only faintly masking a smile. "Well…and you knew her?"

"My sister Etta knew her better."

"You have a sister?"

She nodded. Her eyes were wide and dark with what Edmund mistook for enchantment.

Edmund inched closer to Mr. Ripley Marshall who seemed to be pulling him in like a boat to shore.

"My father died in Cuba."

"That I know, son. I was at his side when he died."

There was a long pause and Edmund caught himself chewing on his tongue.

"What have you heard about your Pap?"

Edmund blinked. "That…he was cut in half by a cannonball."

Mr. Ripley Marshall nodded. "That was a fellow a' named Wilmot. Not Ellicott. Deaver Wilmot. Your Pap was still alive when that happened. It was he and myself that drug that poor boy out of the tall grass. And that was on Kettle Hill. Hadn't even reached San Juan Hill yet."

There was a quietness then, and Jeff edged up to Edmund's side. Both boys looked at Sheriff Ben and then back to Mr. Ripley Marshall.

"Those kinds of misunderstandings are common in war, son. And it's true. Your Pap did die later, on the big hill. We was racing up side-by-side like a pair of draft mules. Us and the whole Rough Riders. It was Teddy leading us on. What a glorious sight. It wasn't glorious at the time—memory's what makes it glorious. We was hot and tired and sick and scared. But the Spaniards was up there, and we was down here and so up we went to meet 'em."

Edmund found himself near to kneeling on the porch boards now. He looked squarely into the man's soft blue eyes, as if he'd been invited there, as if the other side of his young life lay hidden there. And it was.

"We was a sea of blue shirts and suspenders. Shooting while we ran. We ran to meet death."

There was a catch in the man's throat suddenly, and when Edmund looked deeper, he saw a watery reservoir of sadness held back by his eyelids. "'Keep your feet, Rip.' That's what your Pap told me. The tall grass was a bastard to run in. 'Keep your feet.' Then he fell like a stone. No noise, he just plopped like a clod in a plowfield. And I come back to him and saw the bad news."

Finally, Edmund looked away, his eyes now studying the dust between the cracks of the porch boards but not even seeing that, seeing nothing except what his head now held in it—the picture of his father falling like that, so noiselessly and without parade.

"Before I got to him, he had rolled himself over and was preparing to fire his Krag from the ground. But his strength had been all shot out of him. We never hardly did see the Spaniards that day. Not until we had them running out of their cover in the blockhouse and the hedgerows."

This time it was Sheriff Ben who looked at Mr. Ripley Marshall. "He's just a boy."

"I know that. But he has a right to know his Pap's last words. I've held them in myself these years till I figured he was old enough. I hope by passing them on it will rid me of them."

"Tell me," Edmund said. "I ain't afraid."

"They were shooting smokeless powder at us. That prevented us from seeing their hiding places. Had they been shooting the black devil powder our carbines used, it would have been all different. I don't think—never did think—that your Pap taking a bullet that day was anywhere random. He was a target. Your Pap, above all others, was laying down a magnificent fire and them Spaniard bastards knew that he had to fall or they themselves would die."

Off in the distance a dog took up a racket of barking, but nobody looked. Edmund's mouth was partly open.

"I knelt there in the grass and turned him over so I could see his wound, but he grabbed my shirt and pulled me to the ground. 'Git down damn you or they'll kill you too.'"

These words caused Mr. Ripley Marshall to swipe hastily at his eyes as tears left furrows down his brown cheeks, and Edmund's eyes widened at the sight of this.

"The firing was heavy now. Bullets flying thick as hornets." His voice had grown very quiet, and everyone leaned in to hear him. *Ain't it otherwise a pretty fine day.* That's what he said. There's a stain growing red across his breast and old Ellie is talking about the fine day. In truth, it weren't no fine day at all. It was hotter than Satan's nuts. But your Pap just laid there looking up into the sky, the long blades of grass waving in the wind. You'd have thought he was laying on a riverbank somewhere, fishing for perch. But...it wasn't no fishing pole. It was his Krag. It was this Krag, right here."

For the first time, he acknowledged the rifle nestled between his knees.

"Time was getting close, and your Pap knew it. He pushed his Krag into my arms and said, 'I got a boy. Just a little feller. See he gets this, Rip, will ya'? It's all I got to give him.'"

47

The silence returned, and for a long moment, it seemed as if this little party gathered at the jail office were the last remains of humanity on the whole earth. Finally, Mr. Ripley Marshall transferred the rifle into the boy's hands.

"It's a 6.5 mm Krag-Jorgensen Model 1894. The only other person to ever touch this piece besides your Pap was me. I fought bloody hell to get this back to you. Now it's yours, just like your brave Pappy asked."

Edmund took the rifle, timidly at first, and held it afar as if he had been suddenly thrust into the arms of a beautiful girl. His hand stroked the dark wood of the stock. Then the blued steel barrel. And as if by some form of slow magic the importance of this gift reached him, and a stupefying hum left his throat.

"On Kettle Hill are buried no less than three Spaniards that fell because of your Pap's marksmanship."

It took many months for Aunt Delores to satisfy Edmund's request. It took rummaging through long forgotten boxes—boxes that had miraculously survived the fire—before she found a small candy tin that contained several photographs.

Some of the photographs were of Edmund's mother, Agnes, and several were of Agnes and Delores' parents. At last came a photo of his father standing in a bright doorframe in a dark suit and tie. His shirt was as bright as the doorframe, and his hair looked newly combed. It was many years later before a second photograph appeared. This one showed Corporal Titus B. Ellicott standing with several other uniformed men in a half circle; one of the men looked familiar to Edmund because his portrait hung in the schoolhouse alongside the other United States Presidents.

Edmund woke in the middle of the night and thought he saw someone standing in the doorway of his room. At first, he thought it was his father from the photograph. There was a faint light coming in behind him from the corridor, and he wondered why his door was open at all. *Are you sleeping?* The voice had the slurred, drunken tone of Pete Lodge.

It was the night nurse, Theresa.

He lay silent, ignoring her, and after a minute, she left, closing the door behind her. But now he was awake, and for a long time it seemed, Pete Lodge *was* there. It seemed that he had been there the whole time.

Sleep tight, little Eddy.

He remembered the first time he saw the bruises on his mother's arms. She said she had fallen off the ladder at the store. He believed her.

Dovey's face possessed the dreamy detachment Edmund would grow to dread.

"Daddy said he won't be able to come to the wedding. He said he has a mountain of obligations in Buffalo and Albany."

This news came as a relief to Edmund. "Business is business," he said.

"It doesn't have to be big, does it?"

"What? The wedding?"

She nodded.

"I never thought it would be anyway. Just us and probably your brother and a couple of the teachers from my school."

"Maybe my sister could come out from Buffalo."

He shrugged. "If she can make it. It's a long way."

"Bernard might not let her. He's funny that way."

"That's understandable. It's a long way," he said again.

"You'll like Etta."

He smiled, already losing interest in the conversation.

The German sniper hid in the trees, creating a frightful devastation along the lines. It seemed remarkable to Edmund that a sniper would shoot from a place that allowed no escape hatch. If you were spotted in a tree, you were dead.

The rain was biblical. It fell at such a fantastical gray slant that the trench floors could be seen filling visibly, inch by inch. Men were running, bent double, scattering from the intermittent popping of the sniper's destructive fire, scattering from the latest crumbling Tommy. The sniper had such an angle that his bullets seemed to reach right into the earthworks.

Edmund ran against this flow of panicked humanity, directly into the line of fire. He had spotted two muzzle flashes. Separate. But how to get his own muzzle above the parapet to return fire was unknown to him at the moment. His Krag was still wrapped in oilcloth, but the tip of the barrel was two inches exposed. He didn't have time to uncoil the cloth and sight with the scope; it would have to be a quick-kill aim.

As he splashed through the stream of muck bent over, he finally reached a turn in the trench, and without a further thought, he lifted his carbine halfway to his shoulder and sent a single bullet into one of the trees that stood in a dreary cluster a muddy field away.

"You got the sonofabitch," came a shout. It was Ore, somewhere behind him, pressed against the mud with the periscope. A split second later, a return bullet came within an inch of Edmund's ear, striking the muddy trench wall behind him.

Scarcely thinking, he grabbed a helmet from a dead man and tossed it above the parapet. A German bullet pinged it into orbit. Instantly, Edmund rose just enough to send another shot into one of the trees.

"What the hell, man? You got another. That's a hundred yards. How'd you do that?"

"Lucky," someone else muttered, and Ore cursed him into silence.

"'Ey, Ellie," Collins hollered. "There's another one, dropping from 'is tree. Git the bastard."

Edmund rose now, recklessly, pulling the oilcloth away, and with his scope, he sighted the running figure. The trigger. The kick. The German toppled like a man flying.

A stunned pause followed, and then a small cheer went up. Ore leaned his back against the mucky wall and slid down into a squat. Looking at Edmund, he flashed a grave, disbelieving gaze. "Never in my life," he whistled.

It was snowing and Dovey had not come yet. He trudged down the street to the pawnshop and burst in with a cloud of snow following him through the door. From behind the counter, his wife looked at him, amazed to see him so flustered.

"What's wrong?"

"You're usually home by now. I was worried."

She gave him that famous look now, the look pocked with indifference, drained of all passion. In fact, there *was* passion there. It was passion operating in a vacuum—passion derived from a lack of passion. Somewhere inside this strange creature was a river that threw flames onto the shore. A bamboo river— exotic in its inscrutability.

"The store's closed. Why are you still here?"

"I'm just polishing some of the glassware. It gets dusty, believe it or not."

He stood in a stupor, his muffler dangling from his neck.

"I figured you would still be correcting papers," she said.

"I was done by six. It's after eight. And you haven't eaten."

"Max shared his chow mien with me."

"I see." But he didn't see. He didn't see or understand any of it. They had been married for nearly a year, and the oddity of their lives together was equal only to the most bizarre books he had ever read. *Vanity Fair. The Age of Innocence. Wuthering Heights.* "Well, why not get your coat and come home with me now? Surely this work can wait until tomorrow."

"I'll be along later."

"It's snowing heavily."

"I'm from Buffalo, Edmund. I know all about snow."

He shrugged, defeated. "Very well. I'll be home."

Two hours later upon entering the house, she found him asleep on a chair with a book on his lap. In front of the weakening fire, she stripped down to complete nakedness and turned, calling him awake. When he stirred and saw her standing there, she smiled lustily. Lying down on the floor in front of the flame, she opened herself to him. Befuddled, he came to her, and within moments, the small house was filled with her animal cries of desire and fulfillment.

He fell from his bed in the middle of the night, and when he finally found the buzzer and pressed it, he laid on the cold floor for what seemed a long time before the nurse arrived.

"Edmund, what have you gone and done now?"

It was Josephine, and she squatted down beside him to see if he was okay. She put her hand on his chest first and then his forehead, and finally, she asked him if he had any pain.

"A little."

"Where?"

"My hip."

"Oh Lord. I hope you haven't gone and broke your old hip now."

"It's not broke. I can move."

She lifted him slowly to his knees and then to his feet before she guided him back to his bed. He sat on the edge while she inspected him in the dark.

"You're going to have a big old bruise tomorrow. What were you doing, falling out of bed like that? That's not your style now Edmund, honey."

She fixed him back under the blankets and reached down to pull up the rail that swung on a hinge by his bed. "This'll keep you. Here's the cord to your buzzer. You okay now? Look at me."

He stared at her, a small forest creature, eyes shining in the night.

"I'll come and check on you later."

After she left Edmund, stared up at the dark ceiling. He didn't tell her that he had bumped his head.

"Brooke said you fell out of bed last night." It was Katie and she looked at him with blazing blue eyes.

"Did she have to tell the whole damn world?"

"She didn't. She just told me. You're my partner—she wanted me to know."

"Why? In case I started acting crazy?"

Katie shook her head sympathetically.

"I don't have the energy to act crazy. I only know how to act old."

"Stop feeling sorry for yourself."

"Is that what you think?"

"That's what you'd tell me if I fell out of bed. You'd have told me to stop complaining."

Edmund sat ignoring her for a moment, fumbling with his ice cream spoon. Finally, he leaned toward her. "I have a secret."

She looked at him teasingly. "Are you in love with somebody?"

He nodded, his face serious.

"Does she live here?"

Edmund moved closer and raised his finger up and tapped his head. "She lives in here."

"Oh. She's so secret you haven't told anybody?"

"She visited me last night. That's why I fell out of bed."

Katie drew back. "You…had a dream?"

His words came out thick and in a whisper. "All this time I thought she was dead. But she's not."

Katie looked around to see if anybody was watching them. Everyone seemed engrossed in his or her own conversations and Brooke, standing across the room, was writing on a chalkboard, adding to the activities schedule. "I don't think I understand what you're saying, Edmund."

His eyes seemed dreamy. "She hadn't changed. She's still my girl."

"Are…are you talking about someone you knew once?"

He suddenly realized he was being foolish, and he straightened up in his chair and looked away from the probe of Katie's blue stare.

She put her notebook down on the table. Touching his hand she said, "Tell me."

He shook his head.

"Please, I won't tell Brooke. I promise. I won't tell anybody."

Edmund sat like a hawk on a fencepost, erect and proud. "I wasn't always old, missy. You kids think the whole damn world started the day you were born. You all think history is just a bunch of boring dates on a forgotten calendar. I know what you say. I heard it all a thousand times. You think—"

"Edmund, stop. Look at me. I'm going to have to leave in a few minutes. I don't think history is boring. Save that speech for somebody else. I want to know who came to see you last night."

He lifted his eyes and stared into hers. "I…don't know what's real…and what isn't. Not anymore. But I saw her. And she kissed me. She kissed me like she did before."

"Was it Dovey?"

A horrible destruction was ready to spring upon his face, his eyes watery and deep. His chin began to quiver, so Katie reached up and placed her delicate palm upon his face and held it there. Her own heart seemed suddenly ruined with sadness. Sadness for Edmund's sadness.

The white-haired giant from Buffalo wired money to Edmund and Dovey so they could build another room onto their little house. At the time, it seemed unusually generous. And seeing as it came in May, with the summer before him, Edmund was sure he could get the job accomplished in a few months, with the help of some of his friends. After all, it was only a small room. He wouldn't even have to match the roofline with the rest of the house.

He asked his old friend Jeff to help him install an indoor bathroom as well. So they skimped on some of the bedroom materials so he and Jeff could buy water pipes. Together they dug the trench to bury the pipeline, and before long, there was a bathtub and a toilet inside, and Edmund knocked over the old outhouse, burned the wood and filled in the despicable hole.

Dovey watched all this with mild curiosity. She asked him several times who was going to use the extra bedroom and usually he would just shrug. *It was your father's idea.* And she would smile that troubling smile that Edmund mistook as a hint that she might be pregnant. But she was not pregnant, and the bedroom, equipped with a bed and dresser bought cheaply at the pawnshop, sat empty of humankind.

He waited in the dark for her to come back—*her*, his visitor—but she did not come back. Not for a long time.

Edmund was struck by the odd reaction of both Dovey and Maxwell to the news of Bernard's suicide. When he entered the pawnshop that day, asking of his wife's whereabouts, Max was tinkering with something on the counter. Standing there, Edmund saw that it was a revolver. He watched as Max toyed with opening the cylinder, twirling it, snapping it shut, and then repeating the drill. There was no cleaning rag on the counter and no sign of an oil tin, just Max playing with the revolver. He never looked up, only cast his thumb in the direction of the back room.

Likewise, Dovey's expression held no emotion. Sitting on the stool, she was preoccupied with some pointless task. *Etta's husband hung himself.* Later, after they had both gone to bed, he thought it odd that he, Edmund, killer of many men, would be more moved by this absolute stranger's death than those who knew him and supposedly loved him.

For nearly a week, there was no further talk of Bernard. It was as if it had been the news of a flood in some distant land, or a volcano in Asia, where the shock of it is more curiosity than grief. Then, on the following Sunday, as Edmund trudged up the hill from church, he opened the door to find Dovey standing naked by the window.

"Do you have to stand there like that? The neighbors might see you?"

"What neighbors?"

"Worthy Abel can see through the trees now that the leaves are gone."

"Let him see."

"Dovey!"

"What?"

"What do you want?"

"I want you to make love to me. I've been waiting since you left for church."

It was a request he could not refuse. Although her methods were bizarre and the thinking behind them utterly indecipherable, her beauty was never a matter to be overlooked. Standing there in her dark nakedness, her breasts swollen with desire, they fell together on the floor. It was at the very peak of ecstasy that

Dovey, in her quivering, lustful tone, moaned — *I've asked…Etta… to come live with us.*

Aunt Delores and Uncle Victor were waiting in front of the store, watching as Edmund marched up the street toward them, the Krag angled across his shoulder as if he was some youthful warrior returning from the bloody front. When he reached them, he paused and displayed the rifle before him. Uncle Victor stepped forward and put his open hand gently on the top of Edmund's head as if in benediction.

"It was my father's," he said.

Uncle Victor nodded and Aunt Delores, speechless for once, turned and reentered the store.

"My father was not struck down by a cannonball. Not like the stories we heard. He died from a bullet. And his friend, Rip Marshall, was at his side."

Uncle Victor simply nodded again.

Then, over the course of the next few months, Victor began taking Edmund on supply runs to the railroad station at Beaver Pass. They sat side-by-side on canvas pillows, and after awhile, the comfortable creaking of the wagon lulled the words from their silence. Edmund shared with his uncle everything Mr. Ripley Marshall had told him about his "Pap." He spoke of his father's last words, about the rifle, and about how he wanted Rip to give it to "his boy."

"And so, what do you plan on doing with it? With the rifle?"

"I aim to shoot it."

"At what?"

"Tin cans, I reckon. Maybe rabbits."

"So, you want to be a hunter?"

"Sure. I'd like to hunt. Maybe I could kill a deer someday, and we could have venison."

There was a long pause, and for awhile, Edmund worried

that his answers to his uncle's questions may not have been the right ones. When they got to the bridge that divided the counties, Victor pulled back on the reins until the wagon wheels came to a crunchy stop.

Tipping his hat back off his forehead with his thumb, Victor said, "Ain't much other reason to have a gun like that. Hunting may be a good thing. I was younger than you when I was first totting a long rifle. It was my pappy's also. Used in the War Between the States. Reckon that makes you and me kin of a whole different nature."

Edmund beamed broadly. "I reckon."

After they had reached sight of Beaver Pass, Uncle Victor spoke his final words on the subject. "Your father was a sharpshooter, alright. He could knock the eye-tooth out of a tiger if he wanted."

So ended any further talk about Titus B. Ellicott.

"How did you get in with the Canadians if you're a Yank?"

Both men were very cold, and each had blankets wrapped around his shoulders. Edmund had the burned out stub of a cigar in his mouth. Owen's lips had gone blue, and he laughed gently as he shivered.

"I told my first lie," Edmund said.

"Aye, you've got one up on me then." Owen's eyes twinkled in spite of the cold. "I've told a few to myself, I suppose. But never to another."

"I think you might be telling me one now. That would make us even again."

"You're a sharp one," Owen laughed.

"I told you how close I lived to Canada. Why, I stayed in a hotel once. My head was in Minnesota and my feet were in Manitoba."

"Now you're one back ahead of me again."

Edmund wiped at his nose. "I could have lost my citizenship

had I joined straight up. Uncle Sam's pretty pesky about his boys fighting other people's wars."

"So out came the lie, 'eh? 'I be half-French and half-English, and I'll be 'appy to take the oath, Queen Madam'," Owen mocked.

"Something like that. My uncle told the authorities that he could produce my birth certificate, but he'd have to go back and get it. But first, he said, I'd like you to see my nephew shoot."

"There is no question, Lieutenant," Owen said seriously. "You're a killer, alright."

"That's exactly what *they* said. I shot the twigs off a tree at a hundred yards. Then they lined up some pebbles on a fallen log, and when I plucked them off, one-two-three, they stood scratching their heads. They told my uncle to forget the birth certificate. They'd take his word. 'Now say goodbye to yer nephew. He'll be on the boat tomorrow fer training in the Motherland.'"

Owen thought about this for a moment. His eyes moved away, as if he was studying some new form of art in the muddy trench wall. "And now you're here—Tommy at your sides and Jerries to your front. It's a hell of a mix we dragged you into."

"I've been with the French too."

"They must have hated to see you go."

"Everybody's ways are different."

"Including them over there," he said, tipping his head across No Man's Land.

Edmund nodded. "Including them."

They sat quietly for a spell, each trying to decipher the sudden silencing of the guns. Far away the booming picked up again, but it remained still in their sector, and the noise in this absence of noise was deafening. Suddenly Owen said, "Are you literate at all? I mean, do you read?"

"I read."

"You might be the first American I've ever known. Maybe not. I can't be sure. But I am always curious. About books, you know. And what you Yanks are doing—what you're reading. I mean, you toasted Kipling on that first day. Was that a joke for my benefit?"

"Hardly. I was weaned on Mowgli. And Hawkeye."

"Hawkeye?"

"James Fenimore Cooper—*The Last of the Mohicans*. I've read Dickens, too, or had him read to me. Also Melville and Hawthorne. That's what I read."

"What about poetry?"

Edmund thought. "There's Poe and Longfellow. And that fuzzy old fellow, Whitman."

"Fuzzy?"

"Uncle Walt. *Leaves of Grass*."

"Of course. He's the one who's slain the style."

"The very one. But we love him dearly."

Again a mask of contemplation covered Owen's face, and he sat toying with the ends of his mustache, his fingers blue from the cold and his eyes the deep wells of a doubting soul.

"Why do you ask?" Edmund said.

Owen shook himself from his spell but gave no reply.

Dovey had fallen asleep early, stretched across the full of the bed. It was late, but Edmund remained up, staring into the fire. He had a lot on his mind. Ever since hearing about Bernard and then Dovey's pronouncement that her sister was coming to live with them. He resented deeply that it had come as it had, a surprise blurted as such, without the dignity of a discussion between them. Who else had been privy to this decision? Maxwell? Had he known?

His exasperation led him to the outdoors; bundled up, he began the slow, aimless slog toward town. The lights of Smithfield shone yellow against the black of the sky with great heaps of snow on the hills and in amongst the trees.

When he reached the boardwalk, he stopped and sat on the bench outside Cecil Bosyan's grocery store. Everything was closed of course, except the Songbird Tavern and farther beyond, The Paradise. But liquor was not what he sought. Neither was company of any particular kind. Unless he could find somebody who might explain to him what the hell had happened to get him into this mess.

Up again, he strolled quietly along the streets, peering into darkened windows and up shadowed, sinister-looking alleys. As he drew abreast of the pawnshop, he noticed faded green light pouring out of the backroom window. Another poker party, he thought. Instinctively, he turned down the alleyway and walked until he stood directly beneath the window. Already he could hear the muffled voices, and in his mind, he could envision all the faces gathered around the table, poker chips askew, open bottles of whisky and gin, cigars and their smoke.

For a long time, he stood there, feeling foolish and lonely. On impulse, he rolled a rain barrel across the alley and righted it under the window. Grabbing a gutter, he hoisted himself aboard and cautiously peered around the corner of the glass. It was almost exactly as he'd imagined — six players with all the paraphernalia that went with an all-night poker game. The smoke was thick, and at intervals, between puffs, the table was almost obscured from his view by the heavy purple haze.

Edmund only knew two of the men, two besides Maxwell. There was Yancy Blunt, the blacksmith. A relief to his wife that he should be here, he thought. One less beating she had to suffer. Across from Blunt was Kovalesky, the bald-headed Polish-Irishman. Hardened by a billion bad Polish and Irish jokes, he had grown into a good-natured bully who had been thrown out of The Paradise so many times it was difficult to keep track. The others were unknown to Edmund by name, but he had seen them slinking around town, usually not during daylight hours. One he thought was named Pull, or Poole, and he was pretty sure he and the other unknowns were transplants who had followed young Max from Buffalo.

He watched the dealer for a while, expertly flipping the cards across the table; he watched as chips were flung into the center and then the silent concentration of the players, their blinkless serpent eyes menacing and untrusting.

Finally, as silently as he had come upon them, Edmund left.

This was the same year that Natalie was a junior, and the advancement she showed in his English class was remarkable. She had been cajoled out of her timidity by Edmund's patient instruction. *Listen, Natalie, you cannot trust your story to anyone but yourself.* She blinked at him, almost startled that someone would speak to her so tenderly. *From this moment on, I am granting you full permission to create from your own imagination.* She blushed. *Use your life like a sword. Make yourself the heroine.*

He read over her work—essays about Bret Harte and Stephan Crane, and the new book by Hemingway, *A Farewell to Arms.* This last one touched her deeply because at one time, she had expressed she might like to be a nurse. But she was shocked and hated the ending, as any young girl hoping to be a nurse would.

One Saturday he saw her looking in the window of Collier's admiring a pretty dress modeled by a headless mannequin. He watched her for a while and then quietly approached.

"Nice looking, isn't it?" he said.

She spun around, and seeing him, quickly dropped her eyes. He waited, saying nothing until finally she lifted her gaze and smiled embarrassedly at him.

"There's nothing wrong with dreaming," he said.

She wrinkled her nose, thinking about this.

He turned from her and looked at the dress. "It's your color too. It would match your eyes, don't you think?"

Natalie colored.

"And it's not too expensive."

"Yes it is," she blurted.

"It's relative to your wants. That's how people like Collier make money. He buys what he thinks he can sell. He is gambling that you will like it enough to buy it."

"And I would...if..." She frowned, not finishing her sentence.

"Are you in a hurry?" he asked, changing the subject. "Could you walk me to the ice cream parlor? It's a perfect day for a sundae."

"I don't have—"

"It's on me."

"But..."

He started to walk and she followed. At Miller's Drug Store they sat at a round wicker table and ordered strawberry sundaes. In the late afternoon light, he saw that her skin was showing signs of color. Those first months last year, when she was a sophomore, she looked as pale as a minnow. He was pleased to see now that she appeared healthier.

What he knew of her was this—her daddy was a laid-off man of the forest, had made his livelihood in the heydays of timber cutting, but now he drew a small pension for having been injured on the sleds, and since he was partially crippled, he couldn't hold a steady job.

Her mother was long dead, had died of the influenza in 1918 when Natalie was only three. Her only brother, older than she and known by few, was in jail for killing a man's prize bull. It seemed he had been there for a long time now. Some said he had gotten out but fled to Chicago. Other folks said he committed another crime in jail so was serving another term. Either way Natalie's life seemed closed up at both ends.

"I need some help, Natalie," he said. "I've been looking for someone who I think could do the job and, well, frankly, it's you that my mind keeps coming back to."

"A job? Me."

He sighed dramatically. "You know I got married almost two years ago."

She nodded.

"And when you get married, you suddenly realize that there's more to life than just your job. Now don't get me wrong—I love my job. I love teaching. But every day, correcting papers. Well, it cuts into my time with my wife. At times, I'm sure she resents it."

Natalie listened without expression.

"So, I've been thinking about hiring somebody to help me correct papers. Someone trustworthy. Someone I can depend on. But mostly, I need someone smart. Natalie, I think you might just be that person. If you're interested that is."

A funny noise escaped her throat. "Correcting papers," she said with surprise. "I couldn't do that. I'm...I mean...I wouldn't know how."

"Oh, I would train you. And besides, it would be the freshman papers. I think you could handle it."

"But, is that even fair? I mean, what would the principal say?"

"I've already cleared it with him. As long as I check your work, he's okay with it." This last was an atrocious lie, but Edmund didn't care. He was trying to do something worthwhile for this defeated young girl. Old man Barnes would just have to understand. Or maybe he wouldn't even have to know.

The sundaes arrived, and they both looked at them as if they'd forgotten why they were even here. They ate in silence. Every now and then, their eyes would meet and Natalie would flush.

Finally, she said, "Are you sure you think I could do it?"

"I know you could. As long as your daddy didn't mind. You'd have to stay after school for an extra hour."

"Would I be in your room?"

"Yes. I could move in another table so you could spread out."

She looked away contemplatively and then said, "I think I'd like to try."

"Great. But what about your daddy?"

She lowered her eyes. "I'll wait till I see if it works out before I tell him."

They finished up their sundaes and then Edmund said, "I'd like this to be *your* money, Natalie. A girl your age should have a little of her own money."

She gave a half-laugh as if that was a ridiculous notion. But then she remembered the dress and she smiled.

It was 1955. Edmund was fifty-nine years old. He was in St. Paul visiting his old friend Roger Bayless, who was now teaching at the university and nearing retirement. They had enjoyed a midday drink downtown, and then after bidding goodbye, Edmund wandered the streets looking in the shop windows.

He bought a cigar and smoked it in the street as he wandered without aim amidst the bleating horns of Fords and Pontiacs and the electrical hiss of streetcars. After awhile, he stopped in a tavern and drank a beer in a dim corner and tried to read the newspaper in the poor light. That's when he saw the news article. He read it and then tore it from the page and put it in his jacket pocket.

At six o'clock, he ordered and ate a supper of hot roasted turkey and gravy at a diner near the river. Then he meandered across the street to a theater and watched a movie. It was *The Rose Tattoo*. And when Anna Magnani came into focus on the big silvery screen, he sighed — *There she is.*

"You ever watch old movies?"

Katie studied Edmund, his eyes red at the rims, watery blue. "How old do you mean?"

"Old. The forties. Fifties."

"You mean John Wayne?"

"I mean all of them. Bette Davis. Loretta Young. Henry whats-his-name."

Katie shook her head.

"Fonda. Henry Fonda. Who else? Hmm, the guy with all the teeth. Big grin."

Katie stared at him blankly.

"Com'on, you've got to know him. Played the preacher. Gantry. Elmer Gantry."

"Never heard of him."

"That's not who played him. That's the name of the movie. *Elmer Gantry.*"

"I've never heard of any of those people. Except John Wayne."

Edmund wagged his finger. "Well, you should. They were damn good actors. All of them. Hell of a lot better than those pretty faces they got now. Oh, oh—Burt Lancaster. That's him."

Katie put her pen down and fiddled with the sleeves of her sweater. She looked disinterestedly across the room. "Who is that man over there?"

Edmund followed her gaze to a far corner where a man sat alone, outside the circle of Mr. Gallagher's history students. He grunted. "That's just Horseface."

Katie suppressed a shocked giggle. "Shhh."

"Oh, he can't hear. He's deaf as a doorknob."

"Why do you call him Horseface?"

"Haven't you ever seen a horse before? They're both wearing the same good looks."

"You're just being mean."

Edmund shook his head. "That man is a killer."

Now she did laugh. "A killer? I'm sure."

"Can you see that scar? There by his left eye. Wait'll he turns this way. There, see it?"

"No."

"Well it's there. Look closer."

"What about it?"

"I gave him that scar."

"Oh, you did not."

"Sure I did. I'm pretty sure I did."

She got up from her chair and walked across the room, pretending to refill her lemonade glass. As she passed by Gus, she saw the braided skin that twisted like a silkworm away from

66

his left eye. She gave a slight shudder and then hurried back to her seat.

"Did you see it?"

Katie nodded, his eyebrows knitted across her pink forehead. "But…but that's an old scar."

"Of course it's old. I gave it to him in eighteen."

"Eighteen? You mean 1918?"

"The very same."

"Why? What? How did—"

"War, Missy. It was the worst shot I ever made. I should have put it right through that damn eye. And right into that stinking Kraut brain of his."

"Edmund!"

"But now I've got to look at him every day. Sitting there, every morning. Across the room there, sucking on his noodles. Slurping up his black coffee. Look. Look at him. Even now he sits there like a cock rooster. But I—"

"Edmund!"

"What? What'd you want?"

"I want you to keep your voice down. People are looking."

"Let them look. It's time they knew who he was."

Katie picked up her pen again. "Edmund, tell me about Burt Lancaster."

Edmund fluttered suddenly, like a bird at a window. "Huh?"

"Your old movies. I want to know about your old movies."

"Oh, those things." He sat for a moment, collecting himself, his thoughts about Horseface trailing away like a paper in the wind. He looked into Katie's face, his own forehead knitted now. "Oh, I won't forget *her* name," he said finally.

"Whose name, Edmund?"

"Anna Magnani."

"Who was Anna Mag…*nani*?"

Edmund sat for a long minute, his upper body swaying slightly as if he were about to tip over.

"Was she in the old movies?"

He nodded.

Something in the way he looked just then allowed Katie to see past his age-carved visage and glimpse into another world, into an altogether different time. For a moment, his face seemed to shimmer with youthful radiance, and as if in a spell, she stared at him, realizing, with belated amazement, that he too had been young once. As through a window, she saw the way he looked sixty years ago, how he looked when he was in love. It was love that did it. It was love that took away his wrinkles, took away his age.

She was afraid to break the spell so she spoke softly. "Why did you like her, Edmund? Why did you like Anna Magnani? Was she a good actress?"

But the spell *was* broken, and when he let out a heavy sigh, he became old again. And more than old, he looked brokenhearted.

"I have to go, Edmund. Mr. Gallagher is motioning for me to come on."

Edmund was back. Looking at Katie fully now, he reached over and touched her hand with his gnarly fingers. Then he winked, slowly and sadly. "When she was young, she was beautiful."

Edmund sat in his wheelchair in front of his window watching the summer waves roll shoreward, their underbellies white like the milky bellies of fish as they curled beneath the blue of their crests. The faint jingle of the chime made him think of the depot bell the day the train came to Smithfield bearing Dovey's sister, newly widowed Etta Page. He heard it from the school, through the open windows of his classroom, the chuffing of the engines, the metal-on-metal shrieking of the braking wheels.

He narrowed his gaze upon Rudy Cornelson. "If there was a moral to this story then, what is it?"

Cornelson's eyes darted in animal fright.

"I know," said Tram Scully.

"Put your hand down, Scully," Edmund instructed.

The locomotive was belching steam now, and several of the students let their eyes drift to the window.

"Cornelson?"

"Mr. Ellicott, he didn't read it. He never reads the assignments." This from Joyce Pruitt.

"Thank you Joyce. That'll be enough."

He turned his back to the class just long enough to catch a glimpse through the window of a figure—it was Dovey, he knew— standing on the station platform. This also gave Cornelson time to have the answer whispered to him so that when he turned around, Cornelson sat brightly with this new stolen information.

"Never catch fish on Sunday," Cornelson blurted, and the whole class erupted in laughter.

"Sorry, Cornelson. Wrong moral. What bright soul fed you that falsehood?"

Cornelson shot Scully a perturbed look.

Edmund squared his shoulders, joined his hands behind his back, and slowly paced the classroom. When he got to Natalie's desk, he looked down at her open book and saw the pen and ink illustration of a man hunkered beneath a snow-filled tree trying to build a fire. Then he looked up and angled a glance out the window and saw that Dovey was now locked in an embrace with another woman, slightly shorter than her, though older by a year, with the same dark hair.

"Mr. Scott, would you please answer the question, since Mr. Cornelson seems to have lost his way?"

Reggie Scott cleared his throat. "Is it—never build a fire under a tree?"

The two women separated now and seemed to be sizing each other up. The distance was too great to see faces, so he turned back to his class and nodded at Reggie Scott.

"Class. Was there a place in London's story when the man could have—*should have*—stopped what he was doing and calculated the deeper consequences of his actions?"

In the end it was Owen, and his words, which made the war stand up, fully clothed in its stark ugliness.

About once a month, Lieutenant Edmund Ellicott would drift back to the 2nd Manchesters, carrying his oil-clothed Krag, moving like a zephyr through the trenches on his way to another sniper location. His orders, folded and stowed inside an inner pocket of his tunic, gave him the freedom to choose his own locality, his settings, and his targets. He was the best sniper in France, and his reputation oozed across the front like the very mud of the trenches—here today, somewhere else tomorrow. Few knew what he actually looked like; some guessed he was a phantom, that he didn't exist at all, but was only a tale told to terrify the Jerries. Others, the few who had actually witnessed his hawk's eye, his steel nerves, believed he was a god, a reincarnation of King David, the giant killer. But before they could be sure, he was gone, sniping for the French again, or the Aussies, or back with the Canadians.

But on the Beaurevoir-Fonsomme Line, it was Owen who was the god.

Natalie's nose seemed almost to touch the paper, her red pencil occasionally circling a misspelled word or an incomplete sentence. She scored these papers on grammar only, leaving its content to be graded separately by Mr. Ellicott.

Edmund watched her, pleased that she had taken to her *job* so earnestly. And her efforts really had made a difference for him, allowing him more time to wrestle with the junior and senior assignments, their awkward, growing awareness of what literature actually was.

He had taken down the little plaque below his name on the door to his classroom. It had said: *Language Arts*. At his own expense, he had Jeff make him a similar plague that read, instead: *The Art of Language*. Much better, he thought. Let's call it what it is, an art form. Each writer a creator. No two ever the same. Declarative Picassos, he'd told them.

Natalie seemed content behind her little desk, her penciled hand reaching up to pull back a fallen strand of hair from her face. She sensed that his eyes were on her, so she looked up, smiling innocently, but he did not look away. He was proud of this special girl, this special interest he'd taken in her, and the way she had responded. Her writing was becoming so clear now, so perfectly concise, that he wondered if perhaps he might approach C. C. Vance at the *Smithfield Standard* and recommend her for a part-time position as a cub reporter. Maybe next year, when she was a senior. She would only get that much better.

She went back to her work, and Edmund turned his gaze to the window in the direction of the depot. It had been hours since he had watched the train deliver Dovey's sister onto the platform, hours since he had seen them hugging each other and then walking slowly through the long street up to their little house, with Dovey's up-and-down posture rigid as a rake, while Etta seemed smallish and delicate and burdened.

Normally, he would be home soon, telling Natalie that they'd done enough for one day, lowering the windows, closing the drawers to his desk, spinning the globe once for luck, and turning off the lights. But today he lingered, his heart, or soul, or both, harboring some stubborn resistance to entering his own house on this night to meet this new person. This uninvited stranger— uninvited by him anyway. There'd been no discussion on the matter, as if he was a mere hireling. He wasn't in the mood to be cordial. He wasn't in the mood to be a gracious brother-in-law host to this woman who had probably driven her poor, weak husband to suicide. In fact, he didn't want to have to sit through any morbid discussions about how and why Bernard Page did what he did. He no longer cared.

But finally, after another half hour, he did stop Natalie; he did send her home. He had reached into his wallet and given her two crisp dollar bills—her first pay—and he felt almost ashamed of himself for delighting in the way her face lit up at the sight of it. Instead of going home himself though, he dawdled down the street like a vagabond, looking once again in the store window at the dress Natalie hoped to buy and then pausing in the doorway of the barbershop and chatting with Kelly Seams and Nug Raines, as if he didn't have a home at all to go to.

Nug Raines caught up to him at the streetlamp, and, with a crafty murmur, offered him a *wink o' whisky*. After considering it for a moment, he looked ruefully up the street. Edward said, *Sure, why not?* It was, after all, 1932; prohibition had been repealed a year ago. Yet Nug, and many like him, spoke of booze in whispers, as if it was still illegal.

Nug was a small fish who no feds would have wasted their time with anyway, but secretly supplying the needs of the town gave him a feeling of importance. Inside, leaning against the bar—Nug owned The Paradise—Nug gave an artistically profane speech on the stupidity of mules and how his stupid mule, Francine, had graduated at the top of her class for hardheaded futility. But Edmund was barely listening. He was thinking of the home he was avoiding and of all the reasons why that was so. He gazed at the door through which shone the darkening sky, and yet when Nug insisted he have a beer chaser, Edmund simply answered, *Sure, why not?*

From the moment Edmund laid his hands on the Krag, it became his steady companion.

Mr. Ripley Marshall's voice rose like a bolt of velvet as he talked. "We ran up that hill like our balls were on fire. Colonel Teddy on our left, all stretched out like a fullback, legs rising and falling strong as pistons. Your Pap was near five paces in front of me when he took his bullet, and it stood him up straight as a pole. Before he fell he turned back to me and for an instant—not even a full second—his face shown as magnificent as a conqueror."

Magnificent as a conqueror.

Long after, even years after, as Edmund lay hidden in the destroyed cover of a fallen building or behind an uprooted tree, his Krag wrapped and ready, his eye like a grain of lead, he would hear Mr. Ripley Marshall's voice in his ear—Magnificent as a conqueror.

The words grew on him. Once, at fifteen, he'd deliberately taken captive a thesaurus from one of his teacher's shelves and looked up synonyms for *conqueror*. He frowned on the *defeater* and the *subjugator*, not scholarly enough, or clearly too scholarly, but the *vanquisher* had just the right sound, even better than conqueror, he thought. *My father died being a vanquisher.*

So, for the years that followed, Edmund traded town life for the deep woods. A crack shot by then, he started earning his keep, not by spending endless hours in the store, waiting on indecisive, testy customers but rather by providing meat for the table. And not just their own table. Uncle Victor set up a bench in the adjoining shed behind the store, adding saws and knives and several hooks from the ceiling, a long roll of white butcher paper, and a cone of twine. He started cutting up Edmund's deer and elk into quarters and steaks to sell over the counter. Later Victor fastened a tarnished meat grinder to the table and began cranking out ground venison.

Hunting was not a novelty in Smithfield, and certainly not in northern Minnesota, but by the time Edmund was sixteen, no one could keep up with his production. Aunt Delores, conceding failure by then in her attempts to steer him away from the gloom and danger of the woods, began "inventing" a complete wardrobe of sturdy winter clothes for him and for his excursions. Nothing, not even the twenty below zero days could keep Edmund from hauling his Krag out into the wilds.

So she sewed softened deer and elk skins into robes and boots and pantaloons. She made him a wooly hat, complete with earflaps from the hide of a bear and special mittens from rabbit fur, with a customized hole for his trigger finger. Maybe in some fancy store in the cities one could buy such niceties, like a mariner supply company or something, but such places were out of reach and pointless when she had everything she needed right in front of her. Her only fear was that he looked so much like a forest animal himself, she worried he might be the one who got shot.

And in reality, it was a risk.

He remembered losing his strength.

It probably started with the cholesterol medicine. It was listed as one of the possible side effects, that and a slight lowering of concentration. Although it might have started earlier, he didn't notice it until one day when he tried to open a jar of pickles he'd just brought home from the grocery store. Hard as he twisted his grip kept slipping. They were the same pickles, the same jars of sauerkraut, the same peanut butter, he'd been buying for years, but now—*what's this?*—he couldn't get the blasted lid to turn. And it hurt his hand too, cramped his hand.

Undaunted, he attacked it again and again, his pride at stake now, until suddenly it simply popped open as if it had all been just a joke.

Instantly, he felt a tremor. He sat, contemplating. Those words—*just a joke*—came tumbling back through time, somersaulting down that corridor of memory like a rolling barrel, the very echo of the words tumbling with them—and her voice, *her* voice.

"It was just a joke, Edmund," her voice edgy with sinful humor.

But it hadn't been a joke at all. She'd actually meant it. And soon enough he would see where that joke would take them.

"If you're going to get squeamish, I won't tell you."

"I'm fine." But she wasn't. Even her reply was feeble.

"Look here. I forget sometimes you're just a kid."

Katie shook her head in earnest, her straight red hair whirling across her troubled face. "It's not that." But she was silent and could not speak.

After a long pause, Edmund said, "Let's talk about something else. I haven't told you about the night I got stranded in the North Woods. I was only fifteen. That's how old you are, isn't it? Well, I'd been—"

Katie thrust her hand up to stop him. "No. You can tell me about that later. Besides, I'm sixteen, almost seventeen."

They sat in wordless impasse. Around them they could hear old Harvey Spencer's tractor-engine voice giving a putt-putt account of his first ride in an airplane. And Willa Fisher and her five hundred cats back when she lived on the farm, in Iowa, or Ohio, or wherever it was. And not speaking, but lurking in the shadows by the drinking fountain was Horseface, him of the flaming scar and the persistent chime, both of which Edmund hated.

"You said her name was Agnes," Katie spoke, with her voice still jittery but determined.

Edmund looked up at her with a great softness of heart. Here was a gentle child, not much younger than his mother was when she married his father. A sweet girl the way Natalie was sweet. But there was a grit to this one. A grit that Natalie had never possessed. Had she, what happened might never have happened. But Natalie was too sweet on the one hand and too fearful on the other. Unsure of her place on the planet. Even in the cold north, in a going-nowhere town like Smithfield, Natalie had never fully grasped a world beyond. A world away from her father, a world away from guilt and pointless obedience.

But Katie seemed stronger. And, of course, it was a different time now. It was 1988, not the 1930s. Kids were more resilient now. Kids today bounced back from all kinds of things. Divorce. A death in the family. Poverty, even. And Katie, who seemed soft enough on the outside, showed a dogged indefatigability.

For a moment, Edmund felt, in the back of his eyes, the compelling pressure of tears. He was beginning to love this girl, this persistent interviewer, this undeterred tolerator of crabby old men. Yes, he *did* love her, her of the red hair and faint complexion, the happy eyes. He loved her because that was what his life had come to. And he loved her because there were so few left to love.

"Agnes, yes," he said, finally. "I suppose it sounds sad… saying I don't remember her. I was so young. Now I am so old. She seems scarcely more than a postage stamp on my long life."

"I'm ready," Katie said. "I'm ready to hear it."

He was afraid to close his eyes though. Afraid if he did, it would be that night all over again, lying in the back of the wagon. Even now he feared he might smell the wet blanket, hear the popping timbers, see the flying flames as they destroyed his aunt and uncle's frame house. And he feared for the other. He feared for the screams of his mother.

He was afraid to close his eyes, so he fixed them instead on Katie's delicate fingers squeezing her pen, focusing on the slow drag of that pen as she started and stopped and started again, writing down what he was saying.

Pete Lodge was an Indian. He took Agnes to dances at Grange Hall in Bullfork and sometimes over the border to the Veteran's Club in Canada. They'd dance and laugh and drink, and for the first time in five years, she felt alive. Her husband, the damned war hero, killed on San Juan Hill, left her destitute. She had to live with her sister, Delores, and work in the pitiless mercantile, day in and day out so as not to be a charity case. But Pete Lodge made her laugh, and so what if he got drunk and hit her sometimes, he was always sorry for it, always said he didn't mean to and would never do it again. There were lots of other men who roughed up their women. At least she had a man.

76

And his appetite for making love was fierce. He always said, "It's the Indian in me makes me such a great lover. So let's try this. Or this, we could try this." And Agnes, horny as a goose on Sunday morning from five years alone, always said, "Yes, Pete, yes." So on the twelfth of November, when Victor took Delores to an Advent supper at the Lutheran church, Agnes let Pete talk her into being chained to the bedpost of her bed. "It'll be wild," he said. "You'll love it," he said. And she did. Or she must have. But when he was finished with her, he threw kerosene on the bed and lit it.

"My uncle saw the flames from the church. He started running home and told Delores to hurry and bring the wagon."

"Where…where were you?" Katie's voice was a whisper.

"In the house. I was in the house. When Uncle Victor got there, the place was an inferno. Somewhere he got a blanket. He soaked it in the horse trough, threw it over himself, and dove in through a window.

"He found me on the floor. He wrapped both of us in the blanket. Next thing I remember, I'm in the back of the wagon, Aunt Delores telling me to lay still. I could see the sparks flying, shooting red rings of flames into the sky. But even after all of that, my mother was still alive. And her screams were the screams of madness, filling the town of Bullfork. They were the screams of everything in her life that had gone wrong. The screams of eternal folly."

Katie had stopped writing, her face a blank sheet.

"The townspeople found Pete Lodge later that night, half frozen in the snow behind a grove of trees. He had been watching the house burn. Enjoying it, I suppose. But he was passed out from his whisky, so the folks hanged him where he was, too drunk even to know he was being hanged."

Katie was steeling herself, her baby-eyes darting to the ceiling, as if looking for some logic to attach to this horror. But there was none.

"I suspect he woke up in Hell, wondering how he got there so quick."

Later in his bed, Edmund regretted telling her this story. She was, after all, only a kid. Still, she kept coming back, like a stubbornly loyal mutt. Was there something wrong with her? It was more than just a grade in a class now. Or, maybe she was one of those one-in-a-million kids who finally realized the world hadn't begun the day she was born. That was something he was always trying to drill into his student's imaginations—*yes, class, Christopher Columbus actually breathed, just like you. And coughed. And blew his nose, and ate, and pooped, and loved. Amazing, isn't it?*

Maybe that's why Katie—little Strawberry Katie—kept coming back for more. But now, he had to worry about her. Could she take it? He had to be careful, because his story had only begun.

As sleep came, he thought of the house, which was only a smoldering pile of ash by the next day. They moved into the back of the store—Victor, Delores and little Edmund—setting up house as if that had been the plan all along. Starting life over. And so began the happy years, as if all the debts to bad luck had been paid in full and no one needed to ever trouble themselves thinking about bad luck again.

The thought disturbed Edmund as it slowly emerged out of darkness, like a snail inching its way across a field of sludge into the open air. The dimming realization, dim but growing brighter, that the only thing binding him and Dovey together was not affection, not necessarily, nor clingy attachment, not even loyalty, and certainly not shared interests, since he had his school and she her pawnshop. No, what held them together—thinly perhaps but persistently—was sex.

These were truths that he had learned long ago but now returned to him in his near sleep, this medicated-sleeping-pill sleep of the rest home. *The rest home.* Everything rests but the mind. A detached memory dancing back and forth like something that has escaped its leash, no longer tethered to a conformed pattern of day-by-day recounting. No, in old age memory is like an escaped convict, a free thing that no longer answers to a master. It *is* the master. Master of itself, to revisit at will this ridiculous old maker of history who just wants to be at peace. To be at rest in this restless rest home.

The look on Dovey's face when he finally reached home that night, half drunk from Nug's free offerings of whisky and beer, was another of those unreadable expressions that had become her trademark, which doubtless had always been her trademark—a wistful, yet detached look that never seemed to convey her truest feelings. Dovey was a master of shadow-play.

"*Shorry*...I'm late," he said in the silly voice of the stupidly drunk. "*Loshs* of school work. Did...did the train come in? Did your...did your *shister* make it?"

"Yes. Etta arrived but she has retired for the evening."

Retired? He thought, almost giggling. Had she been reading Edith Wharton again?

"Of course, it's probably better that you weren't here." She scanned the ceiling, and then the window, avoiding his eyes at all costs. "She's awfully shy anyway. No point wearing her out on her first day."

Edmund swept the floor with his gaze and saw that there was a thin pool of light leaking from under the door of Etta's room, the same room he and Jeff had added on for what he'd hoped might be their children's room someday but was now occupied by her, this sister. And unless she slept with the lights lit, she was not *retired* at all. In his mind, Edmund could almost hear Dovey saying, "*Oh, quick, Etta! I hear him on the porch. Go in and close the door. I'll tell him you're sleeping.*" It was the exact sort of game Dovey loved to play. Deception. She would have made a good spy. Or a really determined lousy one. A stage actress who displayed a special talent for over-acting.

"I'm sorry," he said again, lying openly. "I so was looking forward…to making her acquaintance," he added, trying his own hand at Wharton.

"It doesn't matter Edmund, really. Besides, I was just on my way to bed myself." Her mouth gaped in a counterfeit yawn. "I left a cold pork chop in the icebox for you. You'll probably want to read for a while anyway."

She had been standing there the whole time with her arms crossed, but as she turned to go, she made a sudden diversion and came to him. "Why don't you sit down? I'll take your shoes off." She said this half pushing him onto the armchair.

He obeyed awkwardly but willingly, and as she bent in front of him to pull at the laces of his shoes, the front of her dress came away and he could see clearly both of her breasts. Another calculated move, he knew. Her efforts to pull on the heels of his shoes caused her breasts to sway like chandeliers, and she seemed, in his mind anyway, to exaggerate this tugging of shoes so as to produce the sexual effect to its fullest. She stood then, reached out and pulled on his earlobe playfully, and then crossed to the bedroom and closed the door.

It was later, in the middle of the night, that Edmund woke to find Dovey on top of him, working her naked body against his. Before coming fully awake, he heard her making her hyena sounds of pleasure, first into his ear but then casting her happy moans into the wide spaces of the room. It seemed apparent that her cries of pleasure were meant for all to hear, her sister in particular.

Collins was holding up a dead rat by its tail, even as several more scurried at his feet.

"Dinner, heh, Ellie?" He laughed at his own joke, which turned next into a raging cough. He was sodden with mud, and Edmund saw that the rain had washed a fat careless louse onto Collins' upper cheek. Edmund reached up and pinched the hideous black thing between his thumb and fingernails.

"What the devil'd you do that for? It was meant for our dessert." He laughed again, and then coughed again. Edmund patted his comrade lovingly on the shoulder. Once he recovered, Collins flung the rat over the parapet to the amusement of Richards and Ore, who were shivering under a pegged-up tarpaulin, a river of rainwater pouring off its corners.

Down the line someone was suddenly shouting. "Look out... look out."

Everyone bent and Richards, throwing himself forward, landed headlong in the muddy trench bottom. Edmund pulled him up by the arm and together they squatted down, their backs against the muck. The man was still yelling, but nobody could tell what the ruckus was about. No sniper shots had been fired. It had to be something else. Just as Edmund and the others looked up, a gray-green duck appeared, half running, half flying, and throwing up a magnificent quacking riot.

Now the man was yelling, *"Stop him, stop him!"* Through the foggy rain, a ghostlike figure lumbered toward them, arms outstretched, his cries absurdly comical. Meanwhile, the duck— which must have brainlessly flown into the trench by mistake— continued its race to freedom. Had it simply flown, it would have escaped, but its panic was too colossal, too unbelievable, even for a duck, and it ran instead like a startled hare. And like a hare, it plowed through the crowd, and men dove in the mud in mad attempts to capture it. In the midst of this mayhem, the yelling man raced, kicking up great waves of murky water. For a moment then, the duck seemed lost, vanished in the chaos, and as the hysterical man shoved his way through fellow chasers, he bumped past Edmund, his arms still outstretched as if he was a cartoon character in a newspaper, a cat chasing a mouse.

They all watched him disappear down the trench and into the

fog. Secretly and wordlessly each soldier wondered if a sniper might not shoot down the man as reward for his foolishness. It took several minutes for order to be restored. Richards, covered with mud from his dive, kicked at the ground in disgust. Ore returned to his seat under his leaky tarpaulin, and Edmund wiped muck from his sleeves from when the crazed man splashed past him. It wasn't until then that Collins gave up one of his curvy grins, and from under his gray and wasted overcoat, he produced the duck, its neck newly wrung.

"Huh! What the bloody 'ell," Richards blurted, dumbfounded.

Collins shrugged, still grinning. "It's an art, mates. And it's in me blood."

Ore beamed. "Collie-boy, if anything 'appens to you, the rest of us will starve to death."

At first, they tried to take the Krag away and force a government issue rifle on him, but he protested viciously, shouting at the officer — *This Krag'll kill ten Germans to your one, sir, and if its in my hands, it'll be twice that number.* They let him keep it, but they kept an eye on him too. He was just another fresh kid or else he would die trying to back up his ridiculous boasts. Either way he was probably lost to them.

April 1915. Among the first Canadians to reach the Western Front, Private Edmund Ellicott crouched horrified along the line at Ypres. Only the day before, the Germans had launched a terrible new weapon — *gas*. He had watched, helpless, as swells of yellowish, pea green clouds drifted into their trenches, instantly strangling half a platoon of unsuspecting comrades. The gas had wafted with the wind from Langemarck where the French had been so surprised by this new terror that they abandoned their line of defense, leaving a gap wide enough for the German's to penetrate. Or try.

Ypres was Edmund's baptism into Hell.

Here was Satan's playground, the first mass slaughter of what would be innumerable slaughters to come. All bravado was lost here. The great blade of the scythe leveled the field in a harvest of youthful blood. No horror worse than this. Again and again into the mouth of the flaming dragon. Wainwright, who had come all the way with him through training in Canada and England, was swept away on the first day. Reese. Macmillan. Seacrest. Crowell. Englehardt. Over the top. Running like a herd of stupid, spooked cows. Bumbling under bulky packs.

Private Ellicott raced. Yes, it was like a race, a broad swath of humanity, straight into the meat-mixer. Across the open field he ran, across the broken grass and ruddy clumps of upturned earth. *Almost there. But where was there? What was he supposed to do if he got there?* Against machine guns, their putt-putt-putt, the Devil's own sniggering laughter.

Suddenly, from nowhere, Lieutenant Beech is there running with him and then, with an outstretched arm, pushes Private Ellicott to the ground. He lands hard in the clay, and the lieutenant falls nearly on top of him. *Breathe, you dumb bastard. Breathe or else you'll faint.* Only then did Edmund realize that, true enough, he had not been breathing, only running. Holding his breath and running into death to escape death.

He came out of his bed as if flying, his left leg becoming tangled in the blankets as he fell. For a long time, he laid there, disoriented.

When the nurse found him, he was delirious with fever. She paged the front desk, and two orderlies brought a gurney.

Breathe, you dumb bastard. Breathe or you'll faint.

The room sang with the crackle of gunfire and chimes.

In his delirium, Edmund saw again dead Frenchmen and dead Moroccans, their bodies bloated like fish, vultures perched on their putrefied limbs, gorging on the yellow-black fleshy remains. Wheat still grew between the furrows gouged by German shells, its green stalks bent against the horrible heat of war.

Tangled in this dream of fever and maybe dying, Private Edmund Ellicott stood before him—before and outside of him— still in the trenches, yet the captain's whistle only a few seconds from loosing its shrill beckon to go Over the Top.

He saw himself in this fever-dream, as if he was observing a stranger. Tall by the standards of the day but not more than five foot ten. Hair short with a distinctive part, unseen beneath his steel helmet. But the high cheekbones were there, and the smallish ears, fine nose, and a pulled handsome pair of lips. The whiskers—almost reddish when his jaw reflected the sun—were new to him, having sprouted with the everyday shaving he'd had to endure in the long months of training in the Canadian armed forces. But in this sight of himself, Edmund, now the old-man-dreamer, shuddered in this terrible remembrance of that day— that awful, awful day.

The day he learned to kill without remorse.

That crimson blade of light across the steel sky and then the whistle and the grunts of the men, the heavy dreadful grunts of men pushing off and over, men who had only just recovered from days of German shellfire, that insanity of infinite pounding. The grunts coming with sighs of relief though, relief to be done with the slaughter of enemy artillery and now into a different kind of slaughter, equally as insane but of a more curious and personal character.

Over the Top—here came the great harvesting sickle in the rattling of machine guns, shearing across the stubble field as if someone had his thumb over the nozzle of a hose, spraying water onto a garden in a widening arc. *And how does God choose?* That was his first thought upon seeing the man closest to him fall, almost immediately over the parapet. *How does God go about His choosing?* But the putt-putt-putt of the machine guns erased all such thinking. Later. Those are thoughts for later.

Foolishly, he has fallen behind a group of boys, prancing like colts through the sawed-off stubble field, even though they'd all been told — *Do not bunch up.* And yet, before he could realize his mistake, they were falling in front of him, these boys, arms thrown wide, rifles twirling like batons out of their grasps, splashes of blood flying out of exit wounds like dollops of heavy red cream. *My God,* he thought. He was nearly stumbling now over their falling bodies, and without a thought, he leapt over them, nearly tangling his outstretched legs in their flailing arms.

It was there that Lieutenant Beech shoved him to the ground. *Breathe, you dumb bastard. Take a breath.* Together, they lay only inches beneath the hailstorm of bullets, and then, with nothing more than a tap on his helmet, Lieutenant Beech said, "*Up we go, Private.*" And up they went. Across the slaughter field, his peripheral finally widening, seeing blurrily how the company had stretched out, many still falling, others walking, many running. But oddly enough, none of them seemed to be shooting.

Edmund the old man saw Edmund the young man lifting his Krag halfway to his shoulder then and firing toward where the machine gun bursts were coming from. But it was only guesswork. The field now was cloaked in the gunpowder smoke of battle, and he could see only the hazy muzzle flashes of the killing machines. He fired the Krag. Fired and fired. And then Lieutenant Beech turned back toward him as if about to give an order, but instead he had the glassy-eyed look of the dead, and slowly his long legs buckled and he crumbled down into an Indian squat, his war over.

The sight of this was horrifying. Now what? Other men who had seen their lieutenant die were falling now, too, not from wounds but from confusion. From fright. Only dimly ahead, through the smoke, he saw the jagged shadowy outline of the German wire and the black rim of their parapet.

Suddenly, as if looking underwater, Edmund saw the blurred

image of his father, Corporeal Titus B. Ellicott—or the ghost of his father—decked in full Rough Rider regalia, moving through the smoky haze, head raised to meet the enemy. *Fight, son,* he was saying. *Fight. Be a vanquisher.* A vanquisher? He blinked, but in instant and bewildered obedience to his father, Edmund lurched forward, shouting in a strange voice, *"Com'on men. Fight. Fight…"* And as he ran, he found himself reaching down and grabbing the tunic collar of a prostrate comrade and pulling him to his feet. *"Shoot your rifle. Fire…"* And then another, grabbing him also by the collar and dragging him up. *"Com'on, fight, man. Fight."*

Across the field they rose and once more stumbled toward the enemy trenches, this time spewing a scattering of gunfire, increasing then, and finally into a full-fledged volley. The smoke thickened, but they were at the wire now. Collins appeared out of the haze with a wire cutter and tore into the rusty spools while bullets circled him like offended wasps.

Some of the Germans were up now, abandoning their own trenches and Edmund's company, those who were left and following him, poured another volley into the escaping Jerries, and it became a rout. Collins had the wire open, and the Canadians dodged through it like rats running the yardarms of a ship. Finally, a regiment of Frenchmen took up the fight and secured the German trenches on the right flank, stretching out for half a mile.

The dead lay everywhere. Krauts mill the smoking field with their arms raised, *kamerad, kamerad,* they bellow in pleading, panicked tones. And two soldiers came up to Edmund and asked, *"What now, sir?"* And he turned, not realizing they were talking to him.

When he opened his eyes, it was Brooke he saw pacing the floor of his hospital room. Her too-cheerful face seemed painted there, as if she was a porcelain doll, adorned with rosy cheeks and tulip lips. She was fumbling with something between her fingers, but Edmund couldn't focus with his cataract-laden eyes. But when she stepped closer to his bed, he saw that it was a stick of gum she was trying with some difficulty to undo so as to release the piece from its aluminum wrapper.

"Oh, Edmund, thank God you're awake." She shoved the freed piece of gum into her mouth, hovering over him. "We were so worried about you."

He felt scolded — *bad dog, bad dog* — as if he had done something wrong by falling out of his bed. Again. "Where…where am I?"

"You're in Kennedy Central. Third floor. Room 321. Slight concussion." She rattled this off as if she was calling Bingo numbers.

It is here that Edmund first noticed that his head seemed heavier than usual, as if anchored by a lead weight. He moaned.

"The doctors want to keep you another night or two. Observation, you know. They want to make sure about the concussion. What happened?" She looked at him closely, not sure he understood anything she said.

Edmund looked at her blankly. "I fell."

"I know you fell, Edmund. Why did you fall?"

He couldn't remember. He wasn't even sure yet if he knew who he was. "I fell," he said again. And then he added, "I think somebody pushed me down."

She rolled her eyes. "Now Edmund, don't be silly."

The next day was Saturday, and Edmund woke with an awful but deserved headache, no thanks to Nug Raines. And no thanks to Dovey, who had annihilated his body with her sexual circus in the middle of the night.

After climbing out of bed, he went into the kitchen only to find Dovey sitting there and with a cup of coffee in front of her at the table. She was dressed for work but did not appear in any hurry to get there. The door to Etta's room was still closed, but the expression on Dovey's face was that of sardonic satisfaction.

"Aren't you going to the shop today? You usually leave by now. Anything wrong?"

"Would you like some coffee?" she asked, ignoring his questions.

He remembered her lusty immodest shrieks of last night and how her sister might have perceived them. Her animal howls were something he had grown accustomed to, but he questioned her timing, the very idea of her wanting to make love on the first night of her sister sleeping in the next room. It struck him as suspicious. She had seemed angry with him at first for being late, but then, in the middle of the night, she must have hatched some new plan. Nothing she did ever followed a pattern, except the calculated pattern of unpredictable actions.

Edmund poured himself a cup of coffee and sat at the table. Together they both stared wordlessly at the unopened door of Etta's room as if it was a stage curtain and she was late for her own first performance.

Uncle Victor, older now but not feeble, watched Edmund cleaning the windows of the store with a bucket of soapy water and a towel. Outside, the empty street appeared waffled through the poorly shaped glass. It was spring and he was helping his uncle with the busy chores of tidying up after another long winter. Every so often, from the back room, came a burst of hymnal humming from Aunt Delores who was giving the store-window curtains a seasonal scrubbing in a tub of water.

"How was school this week?" This was Victor's patented question, which he never failed to ask. It was as if Edmund was still the boy coming home from class and not the actual teacher.

"Fine. We're into *Gatsby* again. The kids seem to like it."

The old man nodded. "There's always someone to hate in that

story."

Edmund nodded in agreement. "Surprisingly, the boys hate Daisy more than they hate Tom Buchanan. And they see Jay Gatsby as a weakling. Someone driven by unmanly emotions."

"You got that from Smithfield boys?"

"Well, not exactly. But in their clumsy way, it's what they meant. Not that Gatsby was strange, not in *that* way. The boys just thought if he really loved Daisy that he ought to have simply taken her. Taken her away from Tom."

"How?"

"You know boys. They never think things through at that age. Their solutions are as primitive as their needs."

He threw more soapy water on a window and then put a bristly brush to it before wiping it with the towel.

"How's your new house guest working out for you?"

Edmund stopped scrubbing and dropped the brush into the bucket. Turning, he eyed his uncle curiously. He knew that Victor did not approve of the situation, thought it had been a setup from the beginning, concocted by the silver-haired giant back in Buffalo. *"There's a rat in this whole business somewhere,"* his uncle had said once, *"and it will show its face soon enough."* And he wasn't simply referring to Etta and her arrival, but to the whole family and the whole family business, the pawnshop in particular. Edmund listened to Victor's sermonizing with thoughtfulness.

"It's only been a week, but she hasn't been any trouble," Edmund said.

Uncle Victor only nodded doubtfully. Edmund came and sat on a stool beside the old man, wiping his wet hands on his pants then running his fingers through his hair. "You haven't seen her? She's not big enough to be a burden."

"No, I haven't," Uncle Victor admitted.

"Well, you ought to come down once in awhile. You could have supper with us some time. You could see for yourself."

Victor was silent for a long time, long enough for Edmund to get up and resume his work at the windows. Finally though, and almost as if he was simply throwing questions up in the air for anybody to answer, he asked, "How many banks have shut their doors since the crash?"

Edmund didn't answer.

"I'll tell you," Victor went on. "The bank here in Bullfork was one of the first to go. And both of Smithfield's banks fell like dominos within three months afterward. You live there. You must see the boards on those windows." He said this without malice, rather like a mathematics teacher might present a problem to his class.

Edmund turned again, facing him.

"And look at our shelves. We've got one, maybe two cans of everything. Our inventory is pitiful and has been for the last three years. It's all we can do to hang on. You know that. You remember what this store used to look like?"

Yes, Edmund did remember, and he nodded in sad agreement.

"But there's one bank that hasn't gone belly up yet. And that's that bank that calls itself a pawnshop. The one your wife and brother-in-law are mixed up in."

"Uncle Victor—"

"Don't tell me you haven't been paying attention, son. I'll wager there's more cash stashed somewhere in that pawnshop than both those banks ever saw between them. Why else would Maxwell be burning lights all hours of the day and night? He's sure not making money selling two-bit guitars and rusty pipe wrenches."

Edmund sighed deeply. He loved this old man. After all, he owed him his life for kicking in the window of that burning house all those years ago and carrying this coughing little body out of that fire. Oh, yes, he loved him all right. Loved him enough to wave off his silly theories. Loved him enough to make light of them. Loved him enough to try and keep him from making too much noise. *Because*...because Edmund knew that Uncle Victor's theories were not silly. Victor's suspicions were Edmund's suspicions. But it was not wise to talk about them. If they were true, they were dangerous truths.

Later, driving home from his uncle's store in Bullfork under a pink gloaming sky, he thought about that morning a week ago, sitting in the kitchen with Dovey, drinking coffee and waiting for that door to open, and what he saw when it finally did.

A chorus of the old slave hymn *The Good Old Way* reached its crescendo, the women singing higher and with more gusto than usual, and Edmund, sitting in the outer edges of a pew, thought he could feel the frosted windows rattling.

He turned slightly, his voice joining-in but only with uncertainty. Across the small church in a far pew, her head bent with her own degree of uncertainty, her chin hidden in the folds of her coat, sat Natalie. She was alone, of course. Her father, Samuel Hemmings, could not be torn from his ramshackle farm for a single day. Hemmings' pitiful farm was his church, and his god was the sunshine when he needed it and rain when he needed that. He would have made a great Buddhist, except Samuel Hemmings didn't know such religions existed. To him, China or India could have been on the moon. His world crept like the creeping vines of the forest, amidst those small pockets of trees where he planted every year his failing crops. That Hemmings continued to allow Natalie to stay in school was wonder enough. Beyond school Natalie was as much a recluse as her father. Bound was more like it.

Com'on sinners, let's go down...down in the river to pray.

After the service, Edmund waited for her outside the church, leaning on the hitching rail and swinging his arms against the cold. Only a handful of people still drove buggies to town. A few more rode horses, Edmund included. He had a car but liked to give D'Artignan a Sunday saunter when he could just for the sake of mild exercise. The horse was old but seemed to beg Edmund with watery eyes for that old companionship.

91

"Good morning, Natalie."

Her eyes came up and she smiled shyly. This was not their environment of comfort. Their shared world was the classroom. There, with the heat radiating from the grate and the smell of chalk dust, fine as a Minnesota mist, they sat comfortably. There they could talk about books and writing. It was their shared interest, and Edmund enjoyed it as much as she seemed to. He had no such outlet with Dovey. Pragmatic was not a word to describe Dovey. Detached would be better.

Actually, he had given this a lot of thought lately—how to define his wife. Before, during their first months of marriage, and because he had nothing to compare it to, life seemed normal. Having differing jobs did not seem unnatural, not until it became apparent that they also had differing interests. She had never read a book in her life, and he had no stomach for store work. He'd grown sour on that years ago. Getting his father's Krag from Mr. Ripley Marshall had set him free.

The same seemed true of Natalie. Her father's farm was a prison. Edmund would like to think that the whole town knew it, but the whole town didn't, because the whole town was trying too hard to survive these difficult times to be worried about some seventeen-year-old girl and the impossible trap she was caught in. To Smithfield, Natalie Hemmings was invisible.

"Did you walk in?" he asked.

She nodded.

He looked at her, enjoying the effect of the icy wind on her cheeks. "I'll walk you back."

"But you have D'Artignan."

"Oh, he'll be happy just to walk. He's like a dog now, content to be on a leash."

She smiled, but they did not speak again until they were away from the rest of the church folks. "I...I didn't see that dress in the window." She spoke sadly. "It's gone."

"It's not gone. I had them put it away." He turned to her awkwardly. "Wouldn't want someone else buying it from under

92

our noses."

She blushed. "You...you didn't have to do that."

Again they walked in silence. She blew on her gloveless fingers. It was early November, and the hard northern winter was in the first stages of locking its jaws. Soon school would be the best place to escape the cold. A few brave winter birds made an attempt at a merry chorus as they walked. Occasionally, the horse would nudge Edmund on the back, and they laughed together at this antic.

Then, unexpectedly, Natalie asked, "What do you think of Billy Shaw?"

The question surprised him. "Billy Shaw. Hmm. Well, I only know him from school. He's in my senior literature class."

"I know that."

"Alright. He's not stupid, if that's what you want to know. So far, he's read all the books I assigned. And his papers aren't bad. Not as good as yours. Why do you want to know about Billy Shaw?"

She lifted her shoulders as if feeling a deeper cold and then relaxed them and took a nervous breath. "He sat by me at lunch last week."

Edmund nodded seriously.

"No one has ever sat by me at lunch before. At least no boy ever did."

"And did he talk to you?"

"A little."

"Was it nice talk? Boys aren't always nice. Especially at that age."

"Neither are girls," she said with conviction. "But yes, it was nice talk. He told me he liked the ribbon in my hair."

"Did he seem nervous?"

She had to think. "Yes, he seemed kind of nervous."

"That's a good sign."

She thought about this for a minute. "He plays basketball."

"I hear he's pretty good." There was a peculiar hint of jealousy in his tone, and it confused him. He knew why Natalie was asking about Billy Shaw. He'd waited for this day. Not necessarily with Billy but with somebody. In fact, in a way he had helped cultivate it. It had actually been his hope, once, in the beginning, the hope that this poor girl might start leading a more normal life, a life away from her haranguing, self-indulgent father. And now, here it was. Somebody—besides himself—had finally noticed her.

"You're his favorite teacher."

"He said that?"

She giggled.

"What else did he say?"

"Well…" Her eyes lowered. "That…he…he wondered if he could see me sometime. Away from…away from school."

"Like where?" He sounded fatherly, and he immediately regretted it, but she seemed not to notice. Just talking about Billy Shaw made Natalie's face seem full of spring, even as the north wind placed a rubicund hue to her face. Edmund, in odd embarrassment, glanced away.

It was the morning of his third day in the hospital. With his eyes closed, he heard her voice in the hallway outside his room.

"Granddaughter?"

"Yes."

Even that one syllable *yes* was detectable. He tried to raise his own voice loud enough to be heard, his old worn-out teacher's voice. "Let her in." But the nurse's squawking was too much to penetrate.

Finally, the girl said, "He's expecting me."

"But he'll be going home today. Can't you wait? He's sleeping."

"I'm not sleeping," he hollered weakly.

"Please," the girl said.

Don't beg, Katie, he thought. Never beg. Except to God. But when he opened his eyes, she was standing by his bed, her

94

blue eyes, her pale skin and freckles a balm to the dingy, airless surroundings. It was as if she'd brought spring with her, and for a moment, he saw Natalie's face alongside Katie's, as if they had come together to visit him.

"I went to the place…to where you live. They said you were here? What's wrong?"

"Someone pushed me out of bed. I fell and hit my head again. I guess."

"Who pushed you?" she said, showing alarmed anger.

Edmund allowed the brief fleck of a smile. "Someone from my past—I don't remember who. I have so many."

"You were dreaming?"

"They don't seem like dreams. They come whether I'm asleep or not."

His mind could pick up detail. Like a magnet held over metal shavings. The way he used to. The way he did in France—taking one reckless scan across a barren, shell-pocked landscape and digesting the aspect of danger. One hasty, calculating glare and then knowing. Knowing that at that precise spot, in that grove, or that mound of earth, or that ruined building, a German machine gunner was slapping at a blue bottle fly, just waiting for Edmund and his Krag to end his life. It seemed a form of concentrated science, this ability to visualize and destroy.

It was midnight and he was standing on the barrel again. The alley beside the pawnshop was unlit and shrouded in gloom. On this night, he had taken the precaution of covering his face with bootblack. In the war, it had been ash that he used. And on the Western Front, there was no shortage of ash. Everything was ash. Or mud.

He allowed his left eye to edge around the glass, but what he saw was not a poker game. In fact, there were only two people in the dimly lit room, Max and the man he believed was Pull,

95

or Poole. The table they had once played poker on was now shoved to the side and on it were stacks of small rectangles the size of bricks, each wrapped in white butcher's paper and tied neatly with grocer's string. Max, with his back to the window, was arranging the wrapped bricks into individual piles. Edmund counted. Sixteen bricks per pile.

"*What are you doing up there, mister?*"

Edmund swung toward the voice. A man stood inside a darkened doorway on the opposite side of the alley.

"What're you up to?"

Edmund jumped from the barrel. "I'm looking for my cat. It jumped up on that window ledge."

"Yer cat my ass. You was spying. I seen you."

"Why would I be spying?"

"You tell me." The voice moved away from the doorway toward him, and Edmund saw that he carried a club of some sort.

"Keep your distance," Edmund warned.

"And what'll you do if I don't? You've been snooping and I don't like snoops."

Edmund shot a glance to his left, into the deeper darkness of the alley. He didn't recall ever looking down this alley in the daytime, so he had no idea what lay at its end. "It's a black cat. Hard to see," he said.

"I'll bet it is," the voice answered. "Why don't you step up here so I can get a look at you?"

"So you can lay that club against my head. No thanks. What are you, some kind of guard?" Edmund took several steps backward, testing his footing.

"I am Gabriel the avenging angel."

Edmund put his hand against the side of the building, hoping he might touch a rake handle or a discarded slab of wood. "I think you're confused. That was Michael, I believe. Gabriel is the one who said, *Fear not.*"

"Ain't you a witty sombitch? We'll see how funny you are when I tap your brains out." The voice had a form now, big and hulking, the perfect lookout. He swung the timber around like a baseball player. "Come and get it," he growled.

It was a game of odds, a game of wits. Edmund did not doubt for one minute that this menace standing before him would hesitate to kill him. He was protecting something, and he believed now that he was part of whatever was in those wrapped bricks. Or, maybe he didn't even know what he was protecting, just that he was protecting something. Max's interests? This man Pull's interests? Whatever they were.

The big man stood in the middle of the alley now, shadows still concealing his face, but then Edmund remembered that his own face was covered in bootblack, and he smiled at this knowledge. If this goon represented Death, Edmund was not afraid, because he had faced Death every day in the trenches. He had killed men face to face many times. In fact, he would like to see this man dead right now. He would like to look down at him, the man's eyes bulging like a dead fish's, the surprise on his face of knowing—*I'm dead*.

Then he remembered the gutter. It was rickety to begin with. Pull that down and he'd have a lance. But before he could even formulate a strategy, he felt, in his slow retreat, his heel striking a plank. Then came a bleat and a rustling of straw. Something alive was shuffling behind him. He prayed it was not another man.

"You can't get out that way," the voice said, laughing. "It's time to go meet the boss."

"You mean the Big Boss? The Jesus Boss?"

Another laugh.

Suddenly, Edmund felt a devastating pain in his right ankle, causing him to cry out. He felt shot. In France, he'd seen dozens of men shot in the foot. Seen many others with both legs blow away and them, flopping on the ground, still trying to walk on feet and legs that weren't there anymore. He pulled his foot forward, but something came dragging with it, as if it had bit him and was holding on. The pain was severe, sharp and centered right behind his ankle.

"It's time to go, mister. I got other work to do. Get out here."

Edmund reached down and felt his fingers wrap around a bowed and angular object. He touched his ankle and felt the blood on his fingers and he knew—*Salvation*.

He remembered the date—April 22, 1915. Chlorine gas. Used first against the French and Canadians. When the French fled, it left a gap in the line. He watched the strange fog move toward him and behind him as well. No escape. At his feet lay a dead man, killed only moments before from a Kraut bullet. Instinctively, he fell to his knees, then lower, onto his stomach, and with a panicked hand, pressed his fingers against the dead man's nostrils. Then, placing his mouth over the dead man's gaping mouth, Edmund blew air into the man. He closed his eyes to the absurdity of it.

Even to his own surprise, Edmund saw the dead man's chest rise, his expired lungs filling with Edmund's own breath. Then he sucked back out, sucking his own breath out of the lungs of the dead man. Clean breath, back and forth. Only by exchanging air with the dead did Edmund live. He knew no one would ever believe this. He didn't believe it himself.

Later, after finding shelter in a stable, he decried himself sharply for not finding out the dead man's name. He would have contacted the soldier's family and told them how brave their son was, saving his life and all. He even considered crawling back out amidst the remaining green floating smog of the gas and looking through the dead man's personals for a name, but he never did. He only left him there, lying on his back, his overused, borrowed lungs silent now. Silent as a collapsed bagpipe.

It came only as a mild surprise to the people of Smithfield that their longtime blacksmith, Yancy Blunt, was dead. He had not been a gentle man. A hard drinker. A regular beater of his wife and a fairly regular resident of the city jail. What did surprise them was how he died. Discovered early in the morning by a young milk-route driver, Blunt was found lying on his back in the alley by the pawnshop, a broken-handled pitchfork protruding from his fat throat.

Back in his own bed. Alone now, no nurses poking needles in his arms, waking him up to probe under his tongue with a wooden Popsicle stick, or pry inside his ear, twisting his flimsy torso around so they could shove unthinkable things up his backside. He hoped he could die before ever going back to another hospital.

And he needed no more sleep. He had slept three days of his life away, those last three days, as if they were not precious at all to him, as if they were merely loose change at the end of a life. What do they know? What do they care?

He wasn't always a skin-bag filled with bones. He was a killer once. If they knew some of the things he'd done, they would have approached his hospital bed as if it was a tiger's cage. With a whip and chair. Like in the circus. They would have been careful with their needles and their plastic bottles that squirted liquids inside him.

It was bright outside, but the attendant had turned the Venetian blinds closed so the light could only leak through in narrow blades. It was a depressing light. What were they protecting him from the sun for? Was there a reason, or were they crazier than he was? The sun. Really. As if he hadn't faced worse than the sun in his life.

There were parts missing now, and he realized it. *Knew* it. It grieved him, but he had to face it. Like the time he fell through the ice. He remembered the feel of the cold and the scrambling, manic way he clawed himself back out through the frozen hole he'd made. But he couldn't remember if it was before the war or after. He couldn't remember which lake either—Minnesota, Land of Ten Thousand Lakes—or if he was alone that day or if someone was with him.

The really frightening part about all this was if he forgot something, would he even know he forgot it? How many memories had already slipped through the cracks? What if he forgot *every*thing? People like him—old people—suffer from that all the time. Dementia they call it. He remembered *that* anyway. Maybe that's what he should do—try and remember everything.

He started doing that with Katie, but that was for her, mostly. He had been rude to her, so he was only trying to make it up to her. Help her with school. After all, he was a teacher. He ought to have known better than to give her a bad time. It wasn't her fault he was old. Then he started doing it because he enjoyed hearing himself talk. About all those old times. Now though, maybe he *needed* to do it. Before he forgot everything. Or before he died.

Edmund thought about this for a while. Not everybody lives to be ninety-two, almost ninety-three. Coming upon him now was the face of Natalie Hemmings, and there seemed to be a confusion of stories, a drowning remembrance, something important fighting for air. He was thinking about the day he fell through the ice, but now it was Natalie who was frozen before him. Was that true?

The doorknob turned and that faint scrapping of wood sounded where he and Jeff had wrestled with setting the doorjamb tightly into its opening. It hung just tight enough to cause a mouse-like squeak when it opened, and it was opening now.

Dovey looked up. There was an unknowable expression on her face, the look of someone in on a joke but trying to keep a straight face. And yet, it wasn't that at all, more a shadow of duplicity, a pleasured look of cruelty, as if this might be the final act to her little theatre of loving-making the night before.

Edmund turned toward the door and saw for the first time this sister, this Etta, whom he wanted desperately to hate, whom, in fact, had been training himself to hate, because she might have—may have—driven her husband to suicide and then had invaded their house uninvited. And yet, with that first look, the nagging blast of preconceived prejudice vanished, and he knew instantly he never would hate her. *Could* never hate her. This creature standing before him was utterly unhateable. A mere slip of a girl, for she seemed nothing more than a girl, had a child's face with a half-smile of timidity pressed on her lips.

Edmund rose from his chair without realizing it and fumbled to pull another chair away from the table for her to sit down. In his ear, he heard Dovey's thrilled purr. Etta came forward, a timid fawn, small nibbling steps on little bare feet. She wore a gleaming white nightshirt that, set against the black of her hair, emitted a radiance so brilliant it was as if a comet were passing through the room.

By the next day, the drugs from the hospital had worn off and he remembered. He remembered what he wanted to forget. It was true. It was Natalie in her new dress. She had come to him at the school.

She took off her worn coat, draped it across a desk and then twirled around for him, showing off the dress, its flattering hem lifting above her knees. Natalie might have applied some rouge to her cheeks to highlight them, or it could simply have been the cold air outside. Either way, he found her radiant and, for once, happy.

"I've never…" She looked at him embarrassedly. "I hope he… Billy…I hope…" She almost moaned.

Edmund smiled. "You look beautiful," he said, knowing she

didn't believe it, though wanting to.

She clutched her fingers together childlike.

"And when does the lucky fellow get to claim you?"

Her hands went down to flatten her already smooth dress-front. "I'm to meet him at Rodale's. He isn't telling me everything." She turned away from him slightly. "Well, since Rodale's has the only fountain in town, probably we'll have a malt first. Maybe."

Edmund nodded approvingly. Natalie talked, and he listened, and then, at the appointed time, she put her coat back on and left the classroom. After a few minutes, he went to the window and looked down, watching as she crossed the icy street and started for Rodale's Emporium.

Halfway there Edmund saw Billy Shaw appear. Billy walked ramrod straight, perhaps out of nervousness, bundled against the cold wind in a calico coat, and then he watched the two of them stop in front of each other, saw Billy Shaw bob his head a few times, beaming, and then took Natalie's hand in his and lead her toward Rodale's.

Edmund saw all of this again in his mind, lying in his bed, its clarity sharp as winter stars.

Dovey saw Edmund sitting on the lip of the toilet dabbing at a wound on his ankle, pressing a gray cloth against his skin and removing it, showing a bloody circle.

"What happened?"

Edmund had not heard her approach. She was looking at his stained sock rolled up beside his shoe.

He didn't look up. "Just an old war wound. Piece of shrapnel working its way out."

She stared curiously at the blood and the puckered skin from where it seemed to dimple. It was as she was turning to go that she spoke, almost casually. "Oh, Edmund," she said. "Max asked if you might stop in today. He wants to talk to you."

He swallowed but continued pressing the cloth against his ankle. Trying to sound casual, he said, "Max? About what?"

Dovey looked in the mirror by the door one last time, feigning a dab at her hair, but Edmund caught her eyes looking past her own reflection toward the kitchen door behind her, where he knew Etta was sitting. She appeared to be studying her sister.

"How should I know?" she said, absently. "He just asked that I tell you. Will you? I mean, will you see him?"

When at last she left the house, he commended himself for thinking so fast. The prong of the pitchfork had entered a small vein and had been bleeding stubbornly. Sitting on the end of the toilet, he felt dizzy with the remembrance of his actual war wounds, and thinking about it caused his skin to prickle and itch.

A kraut bullet had gone into and out of his left thigh, and only a moment later, another bullet hit him in the side, bouncing off his ribs, fracturing several, as it turned out. The two bullets, hitting him almost simultaneously, knocked him to the ground where he instantly passed out. He lay like a dead man for a long time, wrapped in the mud, hearing, amazingly, birdsong over the din of departing battle. Finally, all was silent except for the distant pounding of the big guns. He faintly remembered being lifted and carried, dreamlike, but did not fully waken again until he was in an aid station, somewhere in the rear, the stench of sour blood burning his nostrils.

He was in his bed and he felt—not heard—the heavy footfalls of the night nurse coming down the hall. A small wedge of light knifed across the room when she opened his door. He saw her eye in the door crack, an animal eye, he thought, piercing the darkness of his room to make sure he was in his bed this time and not lying on the floor. She seemed to stay too long, staring too long. He wanted her to leave, but she kept her animal eye to the crack in the door. Maybe she wanted to see if he was still breathing. Maybe she wasn't looking at him. Maybe she was listening.

Finally, when he blinked, she was gone and his room was dark again. It was the darkness of cold, broken memory. The sight of her, as if it was only yesterday. Only this very morning. A placidity of expressionless expression. The howl of silence on her face.

"Was she here today?" It was Billy Shaw, standing in the doorway of Edmund's classroom. "I didn't see her in the lunchroom."

Edmund looked at the boy, tried to gauge the root of his concern. Maybe they had not had such a good time last night. Was he afraid of that? That by Natalie not being in school today it could be a sign of rejection?

"She wasn't in class," Edmund said and he watched as Billy Shaw's eyebrows furrowed. "Did you leave her happy?"

Billy nodded, still capable of a nervous grin.

"So it was a good night then."

"I think so. I mean—yes sir. It seemed like it."

Edmund walked to the window and looked out at the gray sky. Then he removed several books from desktops and returned them to their place on the shelf. "Probably had so much fun she slept late. Maybe her dad had something he wanted her to do. He's done that before."

"I'd like to go out and see her," Billy said. His shoulders sagged, and Edmund thought he seemed unsure of himself.

"Would you like me to go out there with you? I could take some papers out to her."

The boy nodded. "Would you do that?"

"Just give me a few minutes to straighten up in here."

Did you get her home late?
Just how cold was it?

What kind of reception did you get from Natalie's father when you picked her up that evening?

Where did you find her?

All these questions and more were asked, over and over again, at the inquisition.

They trudged up to the yard through the snow, Edmund and Billy Shaw, side-by-side. The ramshackle house with its bleak windows and raw wood siding stood like a black omen in the dusky sky. Even these pink streaks painting the horizon lent no cheer to the forlorn little farmyard. Inside the sad dwelling, a dog barked madly.

Edmund knocked on the door, and the dog barked even more crazily. Billy's eyes were wide, and he shivered from something greater than the bitter cold, as if a hideous hand had been placed on his bare neck.

"Mr. Hemmings," Edmund shouted. "It's me, Mr. Ellicott. Natalie's teacher."

The dog barked at his voice, but no other sound came from the house. Billy stepped back and looked up at the chimney. The thinnest thread of smoke rose up through the bricks.

When Edmund turned away from the door, he saw Billy staring at the snow. At footprints in the snow. Footprints leading from the house toward the leaning tool shed. They exchanged a glance and then took several cautious steps toward the black knob and frozen windowpane of the shed door. Between them and the shed was a stack of chord wood, and they both saw where several blocks of the alder wood had been strewn away from the stack. The footprints stopped at the edge of the shed door, the vacant black face of it yawning open.

They looked at each other and then Edmund said, "Let me go in."

Billy was beginning to shake visibly now.

With the toe of his boot, Edmund pushed the door open farther. He stepped into the darkness, afraid to move, afraid he might step on something. He waited for his eyes to adjust, but they remained dim and unseeing. He pulled off a glove, reached into his coat pocket, and retrieved a box of stick matches. He did not want to light it. More than anything in the world this very moment, he did not want to strike a match. But he did, and under the flare, as it rose like a flower blossom, he saw — nothing. Only a pile of rusty tin cans and several broken down garden tools. Then a noise sounded. Billy's howling cry.

Edmund turned into his pillow. He wished he could suffocate himself. Wished he had the strength to hold the pillow to his own face until he could breathe no more.

Natalie's face held a layer of hoarfrost that made her look angelic. Frost even in her hair. Her eyes were half open and empty, staring down. Empty of all love and hate together. Even fear had been erased from her eyes. The hem of her new dress was pulled over her knees and her worn coat was black with ice, the tips of her fingers barely protruding from beneath the furry cuffs. She was half sitting, half lying behind the shed, on the ground, the collar of her coat pulled away, as if at the last minute, she had suddenly felt hot. Her lips, tender in life, seemed even tenderer now and were formed into whatever her last words might have been.

Billy Shaw fell in the snow at her feet, sobbing. He held her small foot, crying as if he were on the brink of death himself.

Suddenly, behind them, the door to the house creaked open, and the dog sprang from its dark opening and raced toward them, snarling. Edmund quickly picked up a stick and drove it off.

"What're ye doin over there?" The old man stood in pants and suspenders; the front of his pants was stained with urine and yellow-brown grime streaked the front of his filthy shirt. He held a shotgun in his hands.

Billy looked up, and the old man hissed, "You. It was you..."

Edmund walked up to Hemmings, and without a word of

warning, yanked the shotgun from his hands. He opened the breech and let the shells fall to the ground. Then he threw the gun into the snow.

"What in God's name have you done to your daughter?"

Dressing station number twelve behind the trenches. Then a grueling wagon journey to the hospital in Boulogne. *E's got gapers and bleeders*, the voice said. They took shears to his crusty uniform and cut it off. They cleaned him of lice and forced him to drink tea and brandy. Drugged, he woke briefly on the Channel, the sea pitching and the bile rising in his throat. Then, at Dover, an ambulance took Lieutenant Ellicott and all the wounded others—the hoards of others—to the hospital at Norwich. But it was full, so he was transported to a village hospital in Newtyle, where he slept and ate and healed and watched through the open windows the birds of May bending the branches and singing their warless songs.

A letter came to him in late June from a chap in Lancashire Fusiliers. *Owen is in Edinburgh, transferred to Craiglockhart War Hospital. He's got a blighty of the noggin. Poor Owen had a heap of a good show at (crossed out), but was taking the part of a hypnotized rooster when he got back, all but walking in circles. We were stuck for twelve bad days along a railroad siding. If it had a name, I never heard it but it did a bad thing to Owen. To all of us. And Lt. G. of B Company didn't come back at all.*

A week later another letter came to him from Collins. *Don't be fretting, Ellie-Boy, I fetched your Krag from the muck. Got that daisy right here with me. I've cleaned it, and I'll shoot the bloke who touches it.*

"You're not eating your ice cream."

"It hurts my teeth."

"You've got false teeth."

"I still have a couple originals."

Katie pushed his bowl aside and looked at him. He was toying with his bottom plate with his tongue, forcing his false teeth to rise and fall with a clicking sound.

"Is that your new pastime?" she asked.

He shook his head. "A seed. That strawberry ice cream has seeds. I got one under my plate. It rubs."

"When you're done, I want to know more about Owen." She drummed her pencil against her notepad.

Edmund twisted his finger into his mouth between closed lips and finally came up with a satisfied grimace. He looked at her with sagging, red-rimmed eyes, holding a tiny seed on the tip of his finger.

"What happened to him?" she asked.

"You ought to know. It's in the history books."

"Well, I *don't* know. So tell me." She was being testy to match his own testiness.

"You are a...determined girl."

"You wanted to say pushy, didn't you?" Her red hair gleamed. "But that's why you like me."

"Who said I like you?"

She tapped his knuckle with her pencil playfully.

He wrinkled his lips and closed his eyes. A long pause and a deep sigh followed, and when he finally spoke, it was in his usual slow, purposeful style, each word a torture.

"Owen was the most interesting man I ever met. A bit peculiar. But serious. Complex. And at the war hospital, I saw him washed and shaven and with combed hair for the first time. And if he could forgive me for saying so, the most beautiful. Cut like a movie star, he was."

"And he was a poet?"

Edmund nodded. "He was just growing into his poetry then.

It had become his clay. He was molding it."

"What happened to him?"

At that exact moment, Horseface appeared around the corner of the corridor. When Edmund saw him, a cloud darkened his face. Sitting in his wheelchair, he gripped his cane and stamped it roughly on the floor, as if trying to tamp down a thorny mound of bitterness.

What time did your daughter get home?

I don't know.

Why don't you know, Mr. Hemmings?

Because I was in the bed.

Now young Mr. Shaw here said it was early. He said it was barely eight o'clock. He said there was still a light on in your house. And he said that he escorted her all the way to the door and waited while she knocked. Were you awake when she knocked or not?

I might have been.

Mr. Shaw said that the dog barked and that he heard you silence it. He heard you shout it into silence from inside your house. Isn't that correct?

The dog barked. Yes. The dog always barks. I can shout at the dog in my sleep.

But you weren't asleep, were you?

I told you I was in the bed.

Billy Shaw said he stayed with your daughter until she assured him that you were awake and would let her inside. She told him he should go, in case...in case of what, Mr. Hemmings? Was it in case you caused a ruckus? Are you in the habit of causing a ruckus, Mr. Hemmings?

She had work to do. I wanted her home.

And she was home. She was knocking on the door. Why did she have to knock anyway? Why was the door locked when you knew she would be home in a few hours? Are you accustomed to locking your door?

It gets locked sometimes.

 Billy Shaw said that when your daughter approached the door and found it locked, she seemed surprised. She seemed surprised that it was locked. Especially on a night like that. You knew she was coming back, and it was very cold outside.

I needed her at home.

In fact, you always needed her at home. Isn't it the truth, Mr. Hemmings that you were angry with her for going out at all? An attractive, smart young girl who, until that very night, had never gone out in her life. Isn't it the truth that the dress she was wearing was brand new, purchased with her own money? Money she earned from her teacher, Mr. Ellicott. Her first ever job. Her first ever pretty dress. Her first ever date. And yet you resented it so much that you locked her out of her own house in order to punish her. To punish her for something as simple—and normal—as a chocolate malt and a moving picture. You were afraid you would lose her. So you punished her by deliberately locking her out of the house. You ignored her knocks. You ignored her pleas. You let her freeze to death on the bitterest night of the year for nothing more substantial than spite. And now we have Billy Shaw who wrestles with guilt for not staying with her. For not kicking in your door. You heard his testimony. The boy is beside himself. The honor given to your daughter by this young man, who barely knew her, was exceedingly greater than any honor ever shown by you, her own father.

The banging gavel rang through Edmund like a bolt of electricity. It jarred him out of the awfulness of his thoughts. Of all the men he had seen killed in the war, as horrifying as it was, as senseless as it was, that horror and senselessness did not match this. The sight of Natalie, her blossoming loveliness preserved by the cruel and unforgiving north winter and the hideous reason for it shook him with a tremor of deep and absolute mortification.

The jury finds the defendant, Samuel L. Hemmings, guilty of voluntary manslaughter and recommend he be sentenced to twenty years in prison.

He wanted to clear his head. Wanted to be released from it altogether. This steady running of the hour, where a too-long life gets lived again and again, over and over. And there was Katie, shouldering-up like a good little trooper. Tough little sprite, she was. But there was more to come. The bad things. The picking up of the Krag again.

When Edmund walked into the pawnshop later that day, Dovey was at the front counter.

"Max is in the back," was all she said.

Without a word, he circled the counter and opened the door.

"Come in, Edmund. I've been expecting you." Max's voice echoed hollowly from a dim corner.

With Maxwell were two other men, one he had seen before, a man wearing purple pants and a manicured mustache. The other man was seated at the table beside Max. Edmund's eyes went to him first for he carried the most menace. His shoulders were broad and his arms thick, and he had both elbows resting on the table in front of him. He had a toothpick in his mouth, and it seemed to move on its own accord from one end of his mouth to the other. His lips were pulled back in a satisfied smirk.

Max leaned back in his chair while the man in purple pants paced behind him, appearing disinterested.

"A story has reached my ears, Edmund. About your uncle. Victor, isn't it?"

Edmund made no answer, just kept his eyes on the toothpick man.

"Seems he's been talking."

Again, no response from Edmund. The room seemed to be

filling up with contention.

Max twined his fingers together in prayer fashion and allowed a smile of his own, resting his knuckles against his chin. "It isn't good for my little business here to have somebody offering up gossip. About things that a foolish old man sees as suspicious."

The toothpick man's grin widened.

"All I'm asking, Edmund, is that you talk to him. I'm sure that your persuasion would be much gentler than...say, well..."

It was perfectly clear now in Edmund's mind. It was every bit clear. Uncle Victor was in danger because he *was* a danger. The ball of yarn was beginning to unravel.

Without speaking a word, Edmund left the back room. As he passed through the pawnshop, Dovey did not look up, but Edmund's sniper vision saw plainly enough the pencil-line crease of a smile on her otherwise expressionless face.

Edmund was crying. He was sitting in his wheelchair, the middle-aged physical therapist leaning over him like a calculating hawk.

"I'm only trying to help, Mr. Ellicott. It's important that we get strength back in your legs. It's important that you not get dependant on this wheelchair. You were doing so good with your cane before the hospital stay."

"I don't want to walk. I want to die."

The therapist seemed unfazed by this remark. She heard it every day from the older residents. "I don't believe you mean that," she said, without emotion.

Edmund was not crying about walking anyway. Little did she know. He was crying about Owen. It was November 4. He had seen the date on the activities calendar down the hall, and the full meaning of the date seemed to jump off the wall and grab him by the throat.

"Mr. Ellicott, if only..."

Edmund planted his feet, moving them slightly to get a grip, and then with a wobbly twist of his bony backside, he suddenly rose out of his chair, fury showing red through his tears. He was up before the therapist realized. With his right arm, Edmund brushed her aside and out of the way, the force of the action causing her to lose her balance and fall onto the floor. But Edmund did not look back, nor did he care to look back, only lurched ahead like a drunken sailor, without a cane, his arms out at his sides like a featherless bird.

Everyone in the room stopped and stared at Edmund who was circling the farthest table now, thin wisps of hair standing above his head like soft dandelion down. He kept going now, afraid to stop. Then, a dribble of croaky words burst from his lips, faint at first but then building from their own strength, from the strength of the words themselves—*Wear it, sweet friend. Inscribe no date nor deed. But may thy heart-beat kiss it, night and day…*

The therapist was up now and stepping toward him. It became like a game of comic tag. Edmund, showing unexplained vigor, teetered left and right, anger and sadness alone keeping him on his feet, his raised voice becoming a whisper…*until the names grow blurred and fade away.*

Another nurse had arrived, but after two steps, Edmund stopped her with a look. Very calmly then, with tears still glinting his cheeks, his face broken and sorrowful, he said, "He died today. Don't you know?"

"She came out of that room like a newly hatched bird. Distrustful. Hesitant. Wary."

Edmund's eyes were closed, and Katie understood he was seeing it all again through the ages.

"I found that I had stood. Didn't realize I had. But Dovey was very aware that I had stood. To her, it was a signal."

"A signal for what?" Katie asked.

Edmund opened his eyes, surprised to realize that he had been talking. He stared at Katie blankly for a moment. "Etta looked at Dovey first and then at me. There was something about her expression. She had just entered the lion's cage."

"Is that why she seemed unhateable to you?"

Edmund thought. "Partly. But more." He turned his gaze away then, seeming to study the great unknowable. Finally, he touched her hand and said, "In your life, girl, there will be rare moments. Moments when strange new worlds are revealed to you. Be prepared for that. They come unannounced. But you must know that they *do* come."

Katie's soft caterpillar eyebrows knitted, not understanding.

"What happened in that room that morning was like a lid being peeled back. A light seemed to come out of that new bedroom when Etta stepped out of it. And her light, probably unknown to her, seemed at that moment, stronger than Dovey's lack of light."

Sitting perfectly motionless, Katie watched him.

"A sudden remembrance passed before me as I looked at her. The train station the afternoon before. Spying through my classroom window. Watching them embrace on the platform. But now I realized." He said this, tapping his forehead with a bony finger. "*They* didn't embrace. Only Dovey did. Etta's arms remained limp at her sides."

"Did...did Dovey feel what you felt? About Etta's light?"

"I don't know. Dovey's mind was like a millwheel. It only turned in one direction. Her direction. She always felt in complete control."

"But you said Dovey saw you standing up as a signal. What kind of signal?"

"That she *had* me. That her games could start now."

"Her games?"

"Cat. And. Mouse."

"What is that supposed to mean?"

"You'll know. You will. If I live long enough to tell you."

114

"Fine, Edmund. So, what else did you see?"

"I saw instantly...that they were not sisters. Except for that black hair, there was no physical family resemblance. None."

"I'm confused."

"No more than I was. But I said nothing."

Katie picked up her pen and then put it back down. "So..."

"Dovey introduced us, and I pulled a chair out at the table. But Dovey stood up and said she had to get to the shop. She placed her hand on Etta's shoulder, and I noticed a faint recoil. It was like an age-worn reaction. A stiffening. Still, so slight I doubt either of them realized it. They certainly didn't realize that I had noticed."

"Edmund the sniper." Katie said this as a fact, not a question.

"Some traits are difficult to surrender."

"So, if you didn't hate her, did you love her?"

Edmund placed his elbow on the table and gently pressed his fingertips to his forehead. He moved them around lightly as if trying to draw out an answer from the past.

Craiglockhart Army Hospital in Edinburgh took its place as the utmost contradiction to the trenches in France. A formidable structure of stone and windows, placed in peaceful recline among trees and grass and bridges and streams. All these were new to Edmund's eyes—trees and bridges that had not been torn to tatters by constant shelling. Streams that for once did not run red with blood. Grass had replaced the waist-high muck of No Man's Land.

A slight lingering limp from his thigh wound, Lt. Ellicott checked in at the receiving desk, asking for Owen. The richly wooded hallways and dark walnut doors muffled the occasional howl that reminded him that this too was a hospital, one treating the wounds of horror rather than blood.

Owen was in his room, a sparely decorated yet comfortable

space. He sat at a desk, with gray light from a cloudy sky coming in through the window. He was not writing, only sitting there, his gaze trained on the movement of small birds milling on the windowsill. He heard a step and turned.

After a moment of confused focus, he said, "Ellicott. What a surprise."

Edmund was stunned by the fresh, healthy appearance of Owen. His scrubbed features gave a glow of external fitness. The gray eye wells that plagued everyone in the trenches had cleared up, with rest, no doubt. His hair, neatly barbered, had its customary center-crown part, and his cheeks, so often ruddy and coarse from the harshness of trench life, shown now altogether more vigorous. Still, there remained that slight pinch between the handsome eyebrows that told Edmund that Owen's thoughts still ran deep.

"How did you get out of there?" Owen said.

Edmund tapped his thigh and then stepped closer, favoring that leg. "Crossfire, I guess. Took one in the ribs too."

"Well, you are a sight. Are you finished then?"

Edmund shook his head. "Orders have me leaving tomorrow. War's not to be won without me, it appears."

"Nor me."

The whole conversation seemed strained, neither man comfortable in this clean, silent environment. Edmund remembered coming across Owen once in the rear, in some shattered French village. He and several of his men were seated around a splintered table, wine bottles littering the scene, cigarettes lit and smoky, giving off a welcome haze.

"*Ellicott, sit with us,*" Owen had said. He spoke without cheer, though his comrades were in a jolly mood. "*Men, this is Lieutenant Ellicott, first name unknown. Puts more singular terror in the Boche then the lot of us put together.*" It sounded like the speech of a drunken man, but Owen had not been drinking. "*Mr. Ellicott, gentlemen, has, with his faithful Krag, pinned back the eyebrows of— how many, Lieutenant? —fifty of our friendly enemies.*"

Edmund carried the mood on with a laugh. *"I heard there's an Indian out there,"* he said, *"a Canadian Indian at that, who is far better than me. Not only shoots them. He dines on their warm livers."* One of the mates who was drunk, stood clumsily from his chair, tipping it over onto the ground, and then moved close and threw his arm around Edmund. *"If you be a friend of our fine leader 'ere...you be a friend of mine."* And the sod kissed Edmund on the cheek.

Owen saw Edmund smile at the memory and said, "You seem happy."

Edmund nodded. "It's good to see you, sir. Alive, of course. Rested and all."

A vague expression of pleasure passed over Owen too. It held for a moment and then faded. "The war does not leave us though. Not even here."

"It likely never will."

"For any of us," he said solemnly. "By the way, how'd you learn I was here?"

"A chap from your outfit wrote." Edmund pictured the man again, the one who'd given him the sloppy kiss.

"Peacock, no doubt," Owen said. "Did he say how things were?"

Edmund shook his head.

Then Owen pulled forth a drawer from the center of his desk and produced a sheath of papers, decorated with his neat, compact cursive. The writing seemed to Edmund like a work of art in itself—inked lines drawing the eyes in as if they were the telling lifelines written across a man's palms. Some words were crossed out, others totally scribbled into blackness, but each page seemed as beautiful to Edmund as a freshly plowed field.

It was no longer Dovey who came to him in his sleep. It was Etta. He had tried to keep her at bay, away from this sad place. Although she was always young when she came to him, when she stood at his bedside and kissed his forehead. But he knew that she could see him for what he was—an old prune.

There was never any mention of the money. Or the train ride. Or later even. The difficult part. There was only the sweetness of her breath. The sweetness of her words. *I love you, Edmund.*

He did not cry anymore. Not for her. She was safe now. And that was what mattered most.

Dovey had left for the shop, leaving them standing in the kitchen, their unfamiliarity seeming to occupy the space with them. Edmund stared at her bare feet; she stared out the window.

Out there, in the yard, where Etta was looking, a horned lark wound up her melody, the tinkling, high-pitched *tsee-titi*, and the sound of it put foolish notions inside Edmund's head. Too many poems. Larks. Larks. He always associated them with beauty, or love.

"Would...would you like some coffee?" he finally managed to ask. She turned and looked at him but only shook her head slightly. "Well, at least sit down, please. I'll have a cup. There may be a biscuit left. Dovey doesn't bake." In fact, he realized as he said this, that Dovey didn't do much of anything except go to the pawnshop. Or howl at the moon, he thought.

Etta moved gingerly to the chair that Edmund had pulled out for her and sat down cautiously, as if it might be an explosive of some sort.

"She—Dovey, I mean—she has a woman, Helen, comes in once a week or so to dust the place up. Helen bakes. That's why there are biscuits sometimes. Oh, and here they are," he said, opening the pantry door. "Me, I teach school. Literature. High school. But today is Saturday, of course, so..." He suddenly realized he was blathering on stupidly. He stopped mid-sentence and asked her forgiveness. "I'm just...nervous."

She looked at him and nodded.

118

Edmund wished she wouldn't look at him because she caused his tongue to thicken, and his throat to catch. But he could not look away. She was the complete reverse of looking at Dovey. Dovey frightened him—her coldness, her wild unpredictability, her misshapen passion. But Etta? In the five minutes he had known her, he only wanted to be close to her. She offered no threat.

She sat with her folded hands between her knees, forcing down the soft fabric of her white nightgown.

"I hope I'm not out of line by saying, I'm sorry about your husband. I won't speak of it again if it's too painful."

She looked at him again. "I don't mind talking about it."

These were the first words Etta had spoken, but it only made matters worse for Edmund because her voice, to him, was like a music box. *You are acting like a damn idiot*, he thought. But he followed that thought immediately with, *Isn't it wonderful, though?*

This was not like the first time he saw Dovey. It was a spell with her, like the devil masquerading as an angel of light. Seeing Etta now made him realize the mistake he'd made with Dovey. What he saw when he looked into Etta's face was…sadness. Pure, undisguised sadness.

He knew such sadness himself. All his comrades who died in the war. And Natalie, both her own sadness, and the sadness of what happened to her. Even Billy Shaw, whose sadness seemed to walk with him wherever he went, a constant companion. But Dovey? He had never seen her sad. She may have acted sad, in her pouty way, but it was always a show, nothing more. Dovey, Edmund realized, was more of a sadness-maker.

All this came to him in the time it took to butter a biscuit and pour a cup of coffee.

"You look handsome today," Katie said.

"It's the haircut, probably." He dabbed at it with a clumsy hand. "Brooke said she was tired of mistaking me for whats-his-name…ah, Mick Jagger. I was hoping she would have said Frank Sinatra. Or Dean Martin. That Jagger fellow is homelier even than me."

Katie laughed, and the honesty of her youth made Edmund happy.

"Did you get a new shirt too?"

"No. Well, this came from a secret admirer. Brooke said it came in the mail. From someone. No return address. She's probably making it up."

"It looks nice." Katie's eyes gleamed.

"It has snaps instead of buttons. Snaps are easier for me to work. Buttons are no longer my friends. These old fingers just can't do it."

"It's good to see you smiling," she said.

"Well," he lowered his voice, "I've been getting visitors lately. At night. It's always good to talk with old friends."

Katie looked as though she was trying to hold back an expression, but Edmund continued.

"Collins came last night. He was covered in mud, as you might expect. The trenches won't dry out until after the spring rains. Then it'll be so bloody hot, you'd like to sweat to death."

Finally, after ice cream, Katie couldn't stay quiet any longer, and she asked, "What ended up happening to your uncle?" She waited then to see his reaction.

"Oh. Sure—well, they came into some money. Unexpected, you know. So they closed up the store. Or sold it, I forget exactly which. Anyway, they moved down to New Mexico. My aunt's arthritis was in a bad way. Mostly from the cold Minnesota winters. So she claimed. She wanted some sun, she said. Some real sun. Year around. Uncle Victor said he would take her wherever she wanted to go."

"So nothing came from Maxwell's threat?"

Edmund's face sobered but for only an instant and then relaxed. He nodded seriously and then turned and looked at her. "It was settled."

He had watched them carefully. After his meeting with Maxwell, watching them became his primary concern. The man in the purple pants—Poole or Pull—was not Edmund's target. Not yet. He was strictly a businessman, meaning whatever was in the leather satchel that always seemed to be visible in Max's back room; that was the purple pant's man's number one priority. The satchel had been there, open on the table, right beside the wrapped bricks. That was the second time Edmund had looked in the window, the night he pitchforked Blunt the blacksmith. And it had been there again, this time on the floor, when Max had threatened Uncle Victor.

It was the other man, the bull-necked toothpick man. He was Edmund's target. Edmund had seen him several times sitting on a bench in front of the pawnshop, arms crossed over his beefy chest, cigar in his mouth, just watching. But Edmund was watching too. Waiting for the moment when it was decided that they would pay Victor a visit. Edmund wanted to be ready for that.

If all of this had happened any other time, it would have been difficult to protect Uncle Victor. Had it been the fall, or the winter, or even the spring, he would have been in the classroom, teaching. But it was summer. He was outside the school, making an impression of being busy, doing odd appearances here and there. And Dovey's mind seemed a thousand miles away, which was just as well.

The Americans were in the war now, so Edmund had to make his presence known among them. At first, some of the officers wanted to challenge his orders, but it was easy to just slip away into the darkness and not return for a fortnight. By that time, he would have made several kills, and if not the officers, at least the Doughboys knew who he was. Word traveled fast.

How long will he last? That was always the question regarding snipers. Snipers seemed almost to be fighting a shadow war of their own—marksman against marksman. The Germans knew him. And they feared him. He was a phantom. When he had been wounded, the story was that he had been killed, but that he had come back from the dead and was on a killing rampage. Myths were every part of living in the trenches.

The range was long, and he'd kept his muzzle wrapped. One shot would reveal his position, but this was a big one. Through his scope he had seen the insignia of a German major, the fool. Every thirty seconds or so, the idiot would show his full face above the parapet, bobbing like a jolly puppet. But Lieutenant Ellicott wanted this one to be a sure-shot, something that would quake the Jerries' confidence. The Tommies were going over the top in the morning, and a sinker through a Kraut major's temple would shake them up badly.

He wished Collins was here with him, to help him spot. But they had him on the line. That poor lovely would be going over the top with the rest of them at the whistle. *Damn bad luck*, he thought.

Edmund watched until his eyes hurt, and then the major's face, full of self-righteous invincibility, passed along a sandbag, and poof, the Krag barked and the bullet entered and exited the major's temple like an incomplete thought. The officer, too dead to realize it yet, actually turned toward Edmund after the impact and appeared to be staring directly into Edmund's eyes, even though the crown of the officer's head had been blown away.

Kraut bullets followed the muzzle flash, but Edmund was already gone.

The wheat was turning gold, and the harvesters were already in the fields along the lake. The big harvesters would make wide swaths into the sweet grain, dragged on by the long teams of harnessed horses. In summers past, Edmund had helped with this reaping, but he had declined the last several years, choosing instead to camp in the backcountry. He didn't hunt in the summer. That he saved for the winter months when the deer would come down and eat at the haystacks. He knew every hill and canyon, every chasm and cliff in the whole of his county.

On summer days, he just wanted to roam, to be alone with his thoughts. He often brought a book and would dig for new stories or poems to enlighten his students. Steinbeck was writing now. *The Pastures of Heaven. The Long Valley.* Putting a challenge to Hemingway. Faulkner too—*The Sound and the Fury*, already a hit, but too big of a pie for his students to be eaten at once. He favored the older writers. Jack London. Zane Grey. Robert Louis Stevenson. The adventurers. The year his junior class read *The Black Arrow* was one of his fondest memories, the boys full of dash, the girls satisfied by the secret Joanna kept.

But today Edmund was lying in the tall grass at the timberline, watching the road. It was at the moment when the sun made its final fall, the green thickets turning pink with the dusk, and the silhouette of a lone man walking the road, standing out like a black bull's-eye against the glow of sunset.

Threaten my uncle, will you? he thought. *And send this hired thug to do your dirty work?*

It was the toothpick man, and he was right on schedule. Edmund's spy, the faithful Billy Shaw, who now worked the Tieko Lake ferry dock, had passed on the word. The dock was a favorite gathering place for the in and outers, the provincial wayfarers who traveled through Smithfield on assorted business, rather than by train. It was also a place where Cam Duffy kept his chowder shop, open to the comers and goers, and for the loafers and hooligans. Plots were laid out on the dock. Secrets shared. And Billy Shaw, forever loyal to Mr. Ellicott and his former teacher's interests, had the ear of an Artful Dodger.

It seemed far too easy now—the toothpick man, walking down the road like a prize bull, an assassin's smirk decorating his face. He marched next to the high weeds of the road between Smithfield and Bullfork. He was going to pay Uncle Victor a visit, under instructions by Maxwell Palvone, to cut out his tongue. And from where Edmund watched, forty yards away on the high ground, it appeared the unsuspecting assassin was savoring the upcoming assignment.

Edmund held the rifle lovingly, and the Krag was true as ever. The bark. The kick. The slow turning tumble of the target. By the time Edmund reached the body, the toothpick man's death-quiver had ceased. But his eyes, not glassy yet, seemed fashioned into a final bewilderment. It was a clean shot, little blood, and since the brute was nothing but a passing operative of the Palvone machine, his absence would not be missed. Billy Shaw had even heard that the thug's instructions were to disappear afterward anyway. Only Maxwell would know something was amiss when Uncle Victor came into Smithfield, his tongue wagging like always, spouting his suspicions to all who would hear.

"I saw the picture."

"What picture?"

"The picture on Horseface's chest of drawers." He grinned triumphantly.

Katie shot him a hard look. "And when were you in Gus' room?"

"Yesterday. I waited until he went into the barbershop. That takes a long time."

"Edmund, you had no right. I ought to turn you in to Brooke."

"Oh, don't do that. I only wanted to see. He doesn't even know I was in there."

"You ought to be ashamed of yourself."

"Why are you taking his side?"

"I'm not taking his side. But I'm not taking your side either."

Edmund ignored her protests. "You know what I found in there?"

"A picture. You told me."

Edmund thrust a huge nod, his chin almost touching his bony chest. "That's right. A picture of him in uniform. A German uniform."

"The war is over, Edmund. World War II is over too. And Korea. And Vietnam. Edmund, you can't keep doing this to yourself."

"It was him alright. I'd know that face anywhere. Even these seventy-five years later. Face like a horse. German helmet. A feeder-belt of ammo hanging around his neck. Machine gun ammo, it was."

"Edmund, look at me."

He did. It took a minute, but eventually, blinking, he focused, and Katie's soft, pink beauty was like a halter around his neck. He pulled up, sputtering. In six months, she had grown on him like a petunia. "What?" he mumbled.

"Stop picking on Gus. Do you hear? You have no right to sneak in his room. And if you keep doing this, I won't come see you anymore."

He looked at her, startled, the reality of her words hitting him like a punch. He seemed confused. His eyes moistened.

"I thought you wanted to get an A," he said lamely.

"I turned the paper in a month ago, Edmund. I *got* my A. I'm only coming back now because..." She sighed. "Because you're my friend."

He blinked, and then he did cry, the tears falling freely off the reddened brims of his eyes.

She put her arms around him and squeezed him tenderly, her supple, sweet strawberry hair brushing against his ear, and then she was crying.

125

The war seemed a hundred years running, Edmund's convalescence but a blink in time. The trenches were still a sucking bog of mud, and the eyes of the lice-infested men darkened with every day. War had taken on the better part of their lives. He walked along the duckboards of a bomb-damaged trench and watched the men, bent to its repair. They stopped work and looked at him, walking with his Krag, his cape billowing off his back, looking every part the Roman Centurion. They simply stood, a long line of them, helmets caked, filthy faces grave with detachment. Blanched, exhausted stares. For Edmund, it was like looking into the dog kennel of the soon-to-be-destroyed.

Edmund moved on past them, no words exchanged, but he felt their eyes upon him. It was 1918. The blood of four years had soaked the land. Rare was a scratch of land that had not been upturned. It would take a million years, he thought, to grow a tree here again.

There was a tap on the door. Edmund was on his knees in the corner of his classroom, wiping dust from the bottom shelf of books.

"Come on in!" he hollered, expecting it to be Branch Hobbs, the summer handy man whom he had heard banging around downstairs earlier. But when he turned, he saw that it was not Branch, but Etta. He immediately—almost comically—got to his feet, brushing vigorously at the dust of his pant legs. "What a surprise," he said.

"I hope I'm not bothering you? The man down at the door said your room was at the top of the stairs."

He felt his heart rise out of his shirt. He moved over and sat on the corner of a desk. "You are not bothering me. This old room just turned brighter when you came in."

She blushed, "Oh, please."

"Sit down," he said. There were chairs scattered throughout the room, but she stepped to the window instead and looked out. "It's my first day out of the house," she said. "I can't hide in that bedroom forever."

Edmund took this chance to gaze at her. Her hair, not as long as Dovey's but every bit as black, was full and falling where it ended in modest curls. "Well, I feel honored that you decided to end your visit with me."

She turned and gave Edmund a coy smile. "Oh, this is my first stop. And probably my only stop. Who else would I visit? You're the only one I know here."

"There's Dovey and Maxwell."

Her expression darkened.

He sensed her discomfort. "I only meant..."

The kitchen at the house offered limited light, but here, with the bay of windows, the room was vivid, and Edmund was struck by Etta's dark skin. It was healthy and deep. Her eyes were dark, and when she smiled, they became narrow lines that Edmund believed held the hope of yet-unfelt happiness. Even her smile, at its height, seemed turned down at the corners. Below her bottom lip, right at the center of her chin's cleft, there was a half-inch scar. These were the things Edmund looked for—the flaws that weren't flaws at all, rather the personalized maps of faces, making people unique, and in Etta's case, stunningly beautiful. He was losing himself in this young woman's face, and he did not feel the need to bring it to an end.

"It might sound terrible but...I've had quite enough of those two," Etta said.

Ah, Edmund thought, *the first honest words this wounded bird has spoken.*

"I shouldn't say such things, I suppose," she said. "I'm sorry."

But Edmund saw that she was not sorry, and it made him

happy. He laughed mildly. "Etta, if it'll make you feel better, I've had those very same thoughts for over a year now."

She brightened at this. "Really?"

"Doubly, I'm sure."

She laughed. "I doubt that. Though, if you don't mind me saying so, I can't picture you being married to Dovey." She looked away, as if she wanted to end it there but did not—could not. "I can't image Dovey being married to anyone."

Uncanny warmth seemed to seep into the room, and they both welcomed it with an ease of movement. Edmund, realizing he still held his cleaning cloth, began folding it absently, while Etta took small steps toward a map of the United States tacked to the wall. It was left over from his history-teaching days, and she placed the flat of her hand on it and rubbed its smooth surface.

Edmund fidgeted with the cloth, wanting desperately to say something profound, or to ask another question that would open up to him this new creature before him. He decided to blunder ahead. "You're not really Dovey's sister, are you?"

She did not stop touching the map but said, without turning, "No, Edmund. I'm not."

Her dress was simple and fell past her knees, but its faint lavender color and her thin gray sweater made her look all the more lovely having made this confession. Now it was her turn to take a chance.

"The Tuscarora. We are a small tribe. Our people were few and always seemed to be mixed up with other tribes. Like the Oneida, in New York. But our chief roots were with the Iroquois. Our men took the side of the colonists in both the war of Independence and in 1812. These are proud things for my people. That's the history anyway."

Edmund listened like a child, eyes wide, breathless.

"My father still wore the long hair of an Indian. He was a handsome man. He worked as a fishing guide in the Thousand Islands. He would be gone for weeks at a time. When he was home, he did odd jobs. Once in awhile, he would haul wood for

Mr. Wilk Palvone. When he did, he would often take me with him, since I didn't get to see much of him when he was guiding.

"I was ten when I started going with him, and I did it for a year or two. Then one day, he was found dead. Someone had shot him. They said the gun was placed under his chin and that the bullet went upward, into his brain. That meant that someone had gotten close to him. It was determined—not by the police, of course, by my uncles—that it must have been someone he knew. Someone he trusted."

Her tone had remained fixed throughout, unwavering, even with the telling of these horrible truths. But a stab of guilt lanced Edmund, thinking of all the deaths he, himself, had caused, leaving scores of fatherless daughters in his wake. It throbbed, a dull, glowing heartache.

"How did you end up with the Palvones then?"

"I'm not really sure. Things happened. Arrangements that are beyond an eleven-year-old girl to understand. It just happened one day. Dovey was only ten. Maxwell was fifteen or so. Maxwell came to our house one day and picked me up. Papers were exchanged and off we went. Wilk Palvone and his wife, Regina, started introducing me to others as their daughter. I was too confused to argue. Their house is very big—a mansion. In Buffalo. I thought it might be like living in a fairy tale."

"Was it a fairy tale?"

Etta turned finally, looked fully into Edmund's face, and shook her head. "At first it was. My father's death had not fully taken shape in my mind. I felt a little like a showgirl, somebody they pushed to the center. Adopting me after my father was killed made the Palvones look like loving, charitable people. Taking me in and all. And that had been the point. Or part of it. To make a good appearance in the community."

Edmund listened, still as stone.

"There was school, of course. And chores. When they had their big parties, I was used as a serving girl."

"Did Dovey do chores?"

Etta laughed. "No."

"Were you close? You and her. You were, after all, pretty much the same age."

"We have never been close. That's why I was surprised when Dovey asked Wilk Palvone if I could come and live here. After Bernard died."

"Tell me about Bernard. Did you and he have a happy marriage?"

Etta turned back to the map without answering. She stared at the wall as if she had the capacity of seeing through it. And perhaps she could see clear through it to another time.

Edmund sat patiently although uncomfortably. His own thoughts were beginning to churn inside his head, peculiar points that were trying to come together, bits of things, like conversations that mean nothing...until they meant something.

"Did you have to read maps in the war?" Etta asked suddenly.

Edmund had to refocus for this new question. "Yes. Yes, I did. It was crucial. The topography of the Western Front was like a spider's web. One miscalculation and I was caught up in it. Why? Why do you ask that?"

She waited a moment longer, gathering her thoughts. "Do you think reading a map could be the same thing as, say...reading a person's face?"

Edmund liked that comparison. And it made sense. "Yes, Etta. I think it might be."

"What do you see when you read my face?"

He flinched, remembering the thoughts he'd had about her that first morning. Even the ones he'd had this very morning. Fidgeting, he told her about the sadness he saw in her face. "I hope I didn't misread. I mean, I'm sorry for your sadness, if that's what it is, but..." He stopped. Here it was, the very same thing he had wondered about, and the thing he should have known himself, from the beginning.

"Dovey? Maxwell?" she asked.

He had moved from the desk and had been standing by the

window throughout this conversation, giving her an uncrowded space to navigate these raw feelings. But now, as an act of pure recklessness, he moved to where she stood. He wanted to touch her face. He wanted to touch her face so desperately that his arms ached, his fingers burned. "Nothing," he said, finally. "I see nothing in their faces. Their faces are a blank slate."

She turned to him. And they studied each other in dangerous silence. Then her dark eyes seemed to beat back the sadness, and she moved into his embrace.

Dovey was looking at him from across the bedroom. She was naked and parading like a goose in front of the back window. Edmund didn't care anymore. Any lovemaking that went on between them was purely an automation now, a mechanical response, as if switches were thrown and clumsy robots suddenly jumped to life, carried about doing what their wiring had trained them to do. Lately, when he and Dovey brought their bodies together, he'd found himself thinking of Etta instead. He doubted that Etta would ever thresh around like an unbroken horse the way Dovey did, whinnying and kicking up a ruckus.

"I have to go to Buffalo, Edmund. My father needs me for something. I may be gone as long as a week. Will you take care of things here?"

Edmund felt like laughing. Take care of things? When did he *not* take care of things? He'd been taking care of things before he ever married her. Or did she mean Etta? Take care of Etta. And in what way? With Dovey, it was easy to imagine.

"What's up? When are you leaving?"

"Tomorrow. First train out."

"Is Etta going with you?"

She blurted out a cackle. "Of course not. Why would she?"

"I was only wondering. No reason."

"You two getting along okay?" It was a question.

131

Edmund proceeded cautiously. "She's quiet. Most of what we talk about is pretty much over the top. And I've been busy with my reading anyway. We've only visited in the kitchen a few times."

Dovey only nodded, no longer listening.

"Bernard was a husband on paper only."

"What does that mean?" Katie asked.

"It means it was arranged. It means that it was a loveless marriage. Etta hardly knew him."

"What? Why would anyone agree to something so stupid? She was a grown woman, for Pete's sake. If my parents tried to pull a number like that, I'd be gone in ten seconds. What a joke. And does that mean they, like...like...never *did* it?"

Edmund waited for Katie to finish her rant. "Life can be complicated," he said. His teacher's voice was back. "Read a Russian novel if you don't believe me. You want to meet miserable people, try dragging your way through *Anna Karenina* while keeping a happy face."

"Then why all the fuss about him hanging himself? Good riddance, I say."

Katie's face seethed red with anger, and Edmund quietly admired her passion.

"I have to take a trip." He let his words hang in the air for a moment. "Will you be okay here for a couple of days if I leave you alone?" He spoke this to Etta in the kitchen.

She was quiet, thinking. "Are you going to Buffalo too?"

He leaned awkwardly against the doorpost. "I'm following something. Some *thing*. It may be Buffalo. It may not be. Wherever *it* goes, I want to follow it."

132

"You know, you're not making any sense." A thin smile.

He crossed the room then and put his hands on her shoulders. She was seated at the table, so he came around and knelt in front of her. "Strange things are going on here, Etta. They have been for a while now. It could be something. It could be nothing. If I have to leave, it'll probably be tomorrow sometime. And it'll be quick. I mean I won't have a chance to run back here and tell you I'm leaving. Or where I'm going. I'll be catching a train, and I'll have to catch it in a hurry. Trust me. Please."

Her eyes came up, as if by some grand presentiment, some ancient design—a predestined molecule of time that had floated in history, waiting to reach them here and now.

"Edmund."

"What?"

Dovey left on the 8:25 heading east. Two and a half hours later, the purple pants man stood on the depot platform, leather satchel in his hand, waiting for the 11:05 to St. Louis. Edmund saw this from his classroom window where he had spent the entire morning, watching. Things were happening

He waited until Poole had boarded the train. Then he sprinted to the depot, winded. He tapped on the ticket window.

"Where's this train going?"

"Saint Louie. But it leaves right now."

"I need a ticket. Quick! I can't miss it." He shoved folded bills through the window, and the ticket master stared at him stupidly.

"Com'on man."

The man tore a narrow leaf of something, struck it with an inky stamp, took the money and shoved the ticket to Edmund. The train's whistle gave a bellowing howl, and the first weighty chuffs of the wheels followed.

"Baggage?" the ticket master called after him.

"No," Edmund yelled, just reaching the last car and clambering aboard before it rattled out of the station. He found a seat and let out a relieved sigh. *St. Louis*, he thought. *The leather satchel was going to St. Louis.*

All through the night, the boys dragged themselves back, slipping over the parapets and sliding into the dark murk of the trench. Lieutenant Ellicott, just back from combing the edges of a copse of broken plane trees, looking for and finding targets, waited for a sighting of Collins. Ore slipped over, but he had no word of the others. He gave Edmund a hollow stare and moved off to find something to eat. Anything. He would eat a rat if he could catch one.

The wait went on through the night, and when dawn spread its deadly pink across the hellish land, Ore returned and saw that Edmund had not moved. He had found some cigarettes and offered Edmund one, but he declined.

"A bugger it was, sir. A bloomin' bloody bugger. The ends folded in on us, and we was cut off."

Edmund took his helmet off and put his open palms over his face, as if to block out the sight of the rising sun, as if to block out the war, the whole upside-down world. It seemed as if he had known no other place than this. That he had lived no other time but here, in this war, tallying up the totals, his friends who had gone over the top and who never came back.

And he had just gotten word that Owen had been returned to the war.

"I found Richards last night. He's down the line, tryin' to squeeze some chicory out of an old sock. It ain't coffee, but it's hot. I'm sure 'e'd share, sir."

"Sit down, Ore," Edmund said, putting his hands back onto his knees.

Ore obeyed, finding a wobbly ammo box that had served well for six months as a stool.

"Tell me about Collins, will you?"

Ore looked at him. "What'd you want to know?"

"Is he married?"

"That 'e is, sir. A fine lookin' woman too."

Edmund gave Ore a fond nod. "The chap has saved me a couple of times."

"Sure 'e has. 'E's saved us all once or twice, sir."

"I'll take that cigarette now, Ore."

"You bet," he said, removing the tin from his pocket and extending it to Edmund. He took one but did not light it immediately.

"How long do we usually wait?"

It was a difficult question, and Ore tried to swallow away his own wretched gloom. "It's near time, sir. It's near time."

Sitting alone in the dining hall, Edmund stared across space into another time. Earlier he had watched Horseface eat his entire meal without ever taking a bite of his own. When the German rose from his table, he gave Edmund a perplexed stare, a look not only for Edmund, but one, it seemed, turned inward for himself—a puzzle that appeared to be working itself out, but slowly, very slowly.

The train stopped often, angling through Iowa and then southern Illinois, and Edmund used this time to casually work his way through the cars until he was only a berth away from the purple pants man and the leather satchel. He purchased a newspaper from a crier at one of the stops and shielded his face behind news of Hitler building up his army. *For what?* Edmund wondered. But he disliked the bastard, he with his feminine gestures and screaming womanish voice. Meanwhile, the Cubs were suffering a three-game losing streak.

Outside the window, the land rolled freely, and Edmund realized that he had forgotten there was any place in the world besides Smithfield and Bullfork, Minnesota. The cornfields were sights of beauty, as they seemed to cover the earth in their enormity. Tractors rattled up flues of black smoke as they chugged in the fields, and every now and then, he spied the glint of the Mississippi River in the distance. And then he wondered about France, and what it might look like now. Were the trenches still there? Had the farmers returned to their fields? What about the destroyed villages—how could anything recover after such a disgrace?

He dozed and when he woke, it was night. For a moment, he panicked, but then he saw through the dim car that his quarry was still there.

Edmund did not see himself as a necessarily impulsive person, dashing off on a trip like this with flimsy purpose. But he had begun adding up a list of inconsistencies shortly after Etta had arrived, and even though he was not a business-minded type of person, he did appreciate when the sums were equal to their parts. That, and the nagging truth of what Uncle Victor harped on about. It was true. Smithfield had suffered bitterly financially ever since the Crash, and recovery, when there was any, was painfully slow. But Maxwell's stupid little pawnshop had pranced along unscathed.

It couldn't have worked out better though, having Dovey out of town. It gave him the freedom to follow this silly character with the satchel and see if he gave up any secrets.

There was something else too. The idea of building a second bedroom came months *before* Bernard had hanged himself. And the building of it had been Wilk Palvone's own idea from the outset. But why? Was Bernard's suicide planned? Or was it even a suicide? If Maxwell's pawnshop was a front for something else, something bigger, and it was beginning to seem obvious that it was, then so too must everything the Palvones were mixed up in as well. In Buffalo and who knows where else. Etta herself had said they did things to give a false impression of charity. Like her so-called adoption.

The train's shrill whistle broke up Edmund's thinking, as it blared like a strangled pelican through the night air. Saint Louis, dead ahead.

The night became a comforter for him. His misplaced hearing aid — his left one — had all but erased the tingling of the chime. So he removed the other one also whenever he came into his room. Sometimes he would sit in his wheelchair under the light and try and focus on his latest challenge — rereading *Riders of the Purple Sage*. Katie, bless her sweet young heart, had found a large print version in a used bookstore somewhere. He wasn't blind yet, but the large print did help him keep his place.

The story itself was good as ever. Lassiter — *I've just stumbled upon a queer deal*. Zane Grey did not make him think too much. His days of analyzing Tolstoy and Faulkner were over. Now all he wanted was escape, and with Grey, he could ride into the rim rocks of Utah and stay there as long as he wanted.

He had stopped reading the newspaper in the recreation room. Ever since the second big war there seemed no end to such foolishness. Korea. Then Vietnam. Desert Storm was different though. Short and sweet, the way wars should be fought. Keep the damn senators out of it. Besides, someone needed to shut that crazy Iraqi devil up. But war never solved much, he thought. *What passing-bells for these who die as cattle? Only the monstrous anger of the guns. Only the stuttering rifles' rapid rattle, Can patter out their hasty orisons.*

Owen appeared to move inside the room, and Edmund stared hard into the dark corner. Of course he was there. The last night they spoke. Only a few words. *Tomorrow we strike out again*, he'd said, in fatigued resignation. *There's that bloody canal to cross. What's the place called?* Edmund asked. *It's here,* Owen said, looking at some papers. *Of course, the Sambre-Oise Canal. That'll be a bloody trick.*

Edmund's book fell to the floor, and Owen was gone. And he *was* gone.

Steam billowed from the engine and threw its ruffled cloud over the depot platform. Edmund, disembarking, moved cautiously inside the haze, keeping the satchel in constant view without being detected. He was a master of stealthy maneuvering—he had forgotten nothing over the years. The purple pants man appeared to jaunt along merrily, and Edmund wondered if maybe he hadn't placed himself on a pointless snipe hunt.

Poole meandered away from the depot and crisscrossed several streets, finally stopping and standing at the corner of Douglas and Ninth. His gaze went up to an end window on the second floor of the Emerson Hotel, a seedy affair with an old-fashioned running balcony that spanned the width of that upper floor. He held that gaze for a long time. Finally he pulled out his pocket watch, so Edmund did the same. Half-past-eight. This was the first clue that a rendezvous could be in order.

Still he waited, stiff as a cornstalk, looking up at the window. Then, as if on cue, a light came on in that end window and the curtains were parted. A woman's face and upper body shown in the weak light, and staring into the dimness, she and the purple pants man exchanged waves. Satisfied, the curtains fell back into place, and the man and the satchel proceeded to cross the street and enter through the doors of a tavern directly adjacent to the hotel.

Edmund followed him to the tavern door but did not go in, only peered through the smoke and noise trying to locate his subject. He feared he might slip through some back door, determined to conclude his mission, but the man, instead, found the quietest of corners and sat down at a table and placed the satchel snug against his leg. He motioned to a bawdy beer girl and ordered. She bent over and ruffled his hair and then pranced off with a delighted smirk. The purple pants man patted down his hair and turned to watch the crowd.

Outside, Edmund moved into the shadows along the sidewalk, trying to appear casual. He wished he had a cigar or some other prop that would give him a degree of purposeful appearance, but he had none. So he merely stood, leaning against a storefront looking somber and thoughtful. Every few minutes, he peered over the batwings. Finally he saw the same girl bring a steaming plate of food and set it before the satchel man. A moment later, she brought him a large stein of beer, and Edmund watched as the man settled down to eating his supper.

He had already planned his next move. The woman in the window. Who was she? Edmund wanted to slip away and see what he could find out, but what if that table in the rear of the tavern *was* the rendezvous place. He couldn't afford to miss it. Still, he thought, he could probably steal up to that balcony and return in less than five minutes. It could be worth risk.

The hotel lobby was nearly empty, save for a pair of gents stuffing their pipes with tobacco and facing each other over a chessboard. There was no bellman, and the clerk, a bulky, oily man with whiskers, was bent over his own greasy plate of supper. Edmund walked casually to the stairs and pranced the threadbare runner up to the second floor hallway. Past the various rooms there was a door at the end of the hall leading to the balcony. Edmund slipped through it onto the rickety balcony. It creaked miserably beneath his feet so he moved slowly. The last window threw a sickly glow onto the balcony so he quietly went to his knees and crawled.

The curtains had not closed completely, and through their parted cleft, he saw the woman, her figure sweeping across his vision. She was moving from one side of the room to the other, a bustle of motion. Finally, she stopped in front of a mirrored bureau and put her fingers through her hair, dabbing and curetting it to her satisfaction, several long curls webbing her forehead. The woman, barely a girl, was pretty with a second-class beauty. Her hair was blonde, and her features, likewise, were pale. She wore well-defined makeup around her eyes and cheeks and red lipstick staggeringly bright on her full mouth. Edmund, seeing this, assumed the girl was a prostitute. Perhaps she was the purple pants man's reward for a job well done.

Edmund was back at the tavern door minutes later and saw the man sopping up his gravy with a wedge of bread. The satchel remained at his feet.

Lieutenant Edmund Ellicott, with face and hands blackened with ash, slipped over the rampart with the deftness of a snake. He felt naked without his Krag, but he had left it with Ore for safekeeping as it would only be an encumbrance on a mission like this. Instead, he had shoved a pistol into the rear of his waistband. If spotted, his Krag would be of no use; he would be killed in a second. The pistol had been Ore's idea, and Edmund had taken it only on his insistence.

The moon, it seemed, had been shot from the sky years ago, and the stars, in their weeping brightness, were absent behind a blur of hanging smoke and clouds. The big guns, their seldom-silent thunder, sent their chorus of anger into another sector tonight, while the horizon flickered only faintly to the east when each shell exploded.

Edmund moved with a purpose, alligator-walking in a sideways action across No Man's Land. The hideous silhouettes of sunken shell craters gave a deadly aspect to the night, and every now and then, he could hear the buzz of broken conversation coming from the enemy trenches. But he moved along, unnerved by their close proximity.

Suddenly he came upon a body. It lay like an earthen mound

in his path, empty of spirit. He felt the face for features, but it was foreign to him so he next went through the pockets of the uniform, expecting to find a last letter to loved ones, but he found none. Around the dead man's neck Edmund located the identification disk and tore it loose. Someone at home would at least take some form of comfort in having their father-brother-son listed as dead, rather than the convoluted "missing in action."

He crawled on. Another body blocked his progress. Following the same procedure, he quickly retrieved a letter from the man's tunic pocket and then took the disk from him also, shoving them inside his own tunic. A flare suddenly fizzled into the sky, sending up a sulfurous shower of light, so he lay like a dead man, his face jammed into the muck. He waited, long after the flare dissipated, daring not to move. Snipers often shot at dead men who were not really dead men, men who were doing exactly what Edmund was doing now—searching for wounded comrades. And he was fully aware, too, that before the night was over, he might well come face to face with a Kraut doing the same thing as he. That was precisely why Ore had pressed the pistol on him.

Edmund felt he was in the rush of angels, busy dragging souls from bodies, a soft whishing of heaven-bound saints. He felt the batting of their wings against his back—not a terrible thing— and strangely, lying there, he remembered the summer after his mother had perished, standing at dusk in his aunt's garden. A sudden explosion of dragonflies burst from the hollyhocks, hundreds of them, flying toward him and then around him, but never hitting him. He remembered standing there, stupefied and laughing open-mouthed at such an astonishing spectacle.

No one sipping tea in London, or Toronto, or Sydney, or even Berlin, would believe such a thing as angels on the battlefield, but the soldiers would. Almost everyone in the trenches had seen sights they could not explain, No Man's Land giving off an eerie shimmer. Some had even seen Jesus there, bent over the dying. They were things too personal to speak of freely, but such accounts were whispered from the fatigued mouths of the hollow-eyed, worn down by living with death. And there were few doubters.

Edmund found Collins two hours into his search, lying at the base of a crater, one foot submerged in the milky water settled in the bottom. He was lying on his back and his head, helmetless, was in a state of peaceful rest. Edmund put his hand on Collins' forehead and brushed back the crusty hair. He felt a dagger of grief clawing at his heart, and he put his own face deep into the bend of his elbow and gave a tearless sob. *What in the name of God have we done to ourselves?*

He moved close and put his arm around Collins and held him. At the rim of the crater, death-birds perched, hopping in their maniac dance. A defeated rage suddenly filled Edmund. A vein of senselessness seemed to burst somewhere inside him, and he pulled the pistol from the back of his waistband. He waved it, unthinkingly, uncaring, at one of the birds, but before he could fire, a voice stopped him.

"*Mustn't.*"

Edmund's heart nearly stopped from fright. He looked at Collins, and through the darkness, he could see the silky sparkle of his eyes.

"…knew you'd come, Ellie."

"Collins. Collins, you old mate." Edmund was staggered. "How…how bad are you? Tell me where. I'll get you out of here. Hang on…"

"*No.* She's worse…than a bloody blighty. It's through me back, Ellie. I'm dead as a turnip below me neck."

"Never you mind, Collins. It's a small thing. Look. Looky here what I have." He reached inside his tunic and pulled out a small flask. "Here. Take a sip of this. It's brandy. It'll warm you. A gift from Ore." He unscrewed the cap and held the flask to Collins' lips and heard him gulp deeply and then cough. Edmund also took a drink.

"Yee 'ard-'eaded Yank."

"Shut up. We've work to do."

"Ellie. *Listen.*" He swallowed. "'Tis'...okay." He spoke slowly, voice waning. "Dyin' ain't it...it ain't the worst of it. I jist..."

Edmund saw the sheen of tears appear before pouring down from Collins' eyes.

"...only feared I'd die...*alone.* Out here..." he sobbed.

Edmund's heart broke. "Collins. *Please...*let me get you back. We can..."

"Just 'old me, Ellie. Put...put yer 'and on me fore'ead again. Like yee did."

Edmund obeyed. He smoothed Collins' hair, he touched his face tenderly, and he even kissed him on the cheek. He whispered words into his ears, words he had never whispered to another human being in his life. They were the rough, strange words of trench love. Words that no one in a sane world would understand. He whispered his affections into the ugly, war-lit night, long after Collins had died.

It was nearly daylight when Edmund gave the signal to Ore that they were coming in and not to shoot. He had dragged the body the whole way back, and when Ore helped lay the beloved Collins gently onto the duckboards, he threatened bitterly anyone who might carelessly trample on him.

Edmund curled his body like a child in his sleep. But it was not sleep. It was the mouse-work of memory. The secret scurrying of voices and faces.

Who goes there now?

Purple Pants checked his watch again. He was getting anxious, but it seemed to Edmund that it was an agreeable anxiety, something that would prove gratifying. He stood, bent, lifted the satchel, gazed around him as if seeing his surroundings for the first time, and headed back toward the batwings. Edmund ducked into darkness and let the man pass out of the tavern and into the night.

Edmund gave him the room he needed to navigate the side streets, moving farther and farther from the noise and lights of the hotels and bars. But not too far. After crisscrossing a third street, Purple Pants stopped abruptly beneath a hanging sign that advertised, to no great surprise to Edmund, a pawn shop. Poole peered momentarily into the dark window, and then checking his watch again, moved confidently into the alley adjoining the shop. The alley was dark, but Poole moved comfortably about in it, and after finding a small rain barrel, he sat down. He balanced the satchel on his lap and like an obedient boy, waited quietly.

Edmund watched all this from across the street, but now he moved closer in casual haste, clinging to the shadows. Several streets away, a dog barked, and Edmund used the noise to cover his footsteps on the boardwalk and into the concaved entrance to a storefront. He waited there, soundless, listening. He assumed whomever Poole was planning to meet would come by way of this very street, entering the alley in the same way Poole had.

He was not wrong. From the duel window glass of his hiding place, he saw the sidewalk without being detected, and from out of the darkness appeared a man crossing the street. In the poor light, Edmund could only make out that this newcomer was fairly tall, dressed in black slacks, black boots and jacket, and wore a fedora that further shaded his face. When he headed directly into the alley, Edmund also saw that the stranger sported a good-size beard.

Like a cat, Edmund crept to the corner of the alley, and with great care, he edged his face to the corner. It was dark in the alley, but he saw that Poole had come up from the rain barrel for this newcomer and that the silhouettes of both men stood facing each other. Fearing detection, Edmund lowered himself to his knees, and then onto his stomach. He inched forward for a better view.

Muffled laughter.

Edmund saw the newcomer take the satchel and then put it down again. He patted Poole on the shoulder and more muffled laughter. Then abruptly a match was struck, the flare bright and crackling, and Edmund saw Poole putting a cigar in his mouth. The bearded man laughed again, and then, with the match still lit, still revealing Poole's face, a pistol was suddenly thrust under Poole's chin and Poole's eyes, wide now as walnuts, he said, "*What, no...Do—*" The pistol's discharge was deafening.

Poole's head snapped back, and he fell over the rain barrel, crumbling against the wall like a rag doll.

Edmund nearly bit off his tongue in shock. He hoisted himself up clumsily, heart pounding, and made an effort to get back inside the alcove of the storefront. He ducked in, shaking, just as the bearded man emerged from the alley carrying the satchel, looked right and left, and then preceded to retrace the route that Poole and Edmund had taken from the hotel.

Poole, the purple pants man, was dead.. Of that there was no mistaking. And Edmund knew he needed to get away from the body in case someone was aroused by the gunshot. But the satchel. He had come to follow the satchel. And now it was moving away from him. He had to follow it.

His curtains were pulled back, and he sat in his wheelchair looking out the window. It was barely light, but Edmund could see the storm waves smashing the rocky coastal cliffs, the foamy spray soaring in the air. *Maine*, he thought. *Not a bad place to go out.* The wind was wreaking havoc with Horseface's chime, its dangling, jangling music, both horrifying and dramatic, reminded Edmund of how Tchaikovsky's cymbals and drums struck out the ghastly rhythms of battle. He had played that symphony on the phonograph in his classroom during the reading of the war poems. Sassoon. Blunden. Graves. And Owen.

The sky was the color of gunmetal, and the rain, as gray as

the sky, came off and on in sheets. It rained like that in Flanders too. Filling the trenches with murky water and turning No Man's Land into a sickly, rubbery swamp. He thought about Collins, and how that thick, loveable bloke never complained. *Laddies, you can fill yer 'ands with complaints and ye still 'ave nothin'*, he said cheerily. *Tis' a bloody picnic, boys. 'ow's about we make the most of it.*

Even without his hearing aids, the storm filled Edmund's ears, loud and wonderful, and the lines of his face lengthened into a whimsical smile. *God has come to say 'is piece*, Collins said when the big guns roared. *Get out the 'ammer, Jesus, me Son, I'm fixin' to pound the lot of 'em.*

Edmund felt the sudden urge to pray, but his faltering thoughts came out confused and silly. Trying again, he gave a slow rendering of *Thy will be done.*

Edmund was clearly no stranger to death. But the scene he had just witnessed in the alley had shaken him. Poole, there one minute, and then the next, executed. And as he trailed the bearded man with the satchel, he was dogged by something else, something the assassin had done, the way he had done it. Putting the pistol under Poole's chin. Not a random move, rather deliberate. The sharp barrel of the pistol lifting the chin back and then...

The man was heading directly for the hotel, the same hotel where the woman had appeared in the window—the girl who had waved. Through the hotel doors he went, across the lobby, and then up the stairs, almost jauntily, swinging the satchel. And Edmund knew then where he was going. Coming in behind him, Edmund watched from the bottom of the stairs as the bearded man disappeared down the hall, and then he heard the click of the girl's door closing.

Edmund wasted no time getting up to the creaky balcony and back to his previous hiding place under the window. The crease in the curtains was still there, and as he cautiously peered through the glass, he saw the bearded man standing before the girl. She appeared fidgety with joy at seeing him, placing her open hands upon his chest. The man gave a satisfied, high-pitched laugh. Then he set the satchel down on the floor and took the girl in his arms and gave her a lengthy kiss full on the mouth.

Edmund watched. But what he saw next, he could hardly believe. After the kiss, the man took off his fedora and flung it into a corner. As he did this, a cascade of black hair fell down to his neck. In an instant, the beard was torn off and dropped to the floor like a furry animal. Then, grabbing hold of his shirtfront, he tore it open, buttons flying, and there, exposed to the girl, were two pale breasts, the ginger nipples tight with excitement. They were female breasts. The bearded man was a woman. The girl touched the breasts, fondling them, and then when they turned, Edmund saw that the woman was—*Dovey*.

The heat of fear rose through Edmund like a rocket. More fear even than going over the top. Nearly crippled with disbelief, he pushed himself away from the window, trying to keep his breathing in check. Still he sounded like a panting horse, like D'Artagnan, in his old age. Edmund felt like running. And before he realized it, he found himself descending the hotel staircase, overcome with this new and terrible understanding. He had just witnessed his wife murder another man. And then, within minutes, he saw her making love to another woman.

He made it to the door and then stopped. *Wake up*, he said, shaking himself. *Push past it.* He was in a war again. A different war. *Think*, he demanded. *Think…*

His eye fell on a coat tree positioned in the corner of the lobby. Two coats hung there, but beneath them was an umbrella caddy. Inside was a lone umbrella, its curved handle upward. *The satchel.* Edmund grabbed the umbrella and headed back up the stairs and to the balcony. When he looked through the curtains again, he just caught the retreating backsides of the two women, naked now, their destination the bed, which Edmund could just see the corner of behind the folding screen.

Forget Dovey for now, he thought. *Think about why you came.*

Edmund knew very well what would follow. And seeing that the satchel was still there on the floor, he knew what he had to do. Very carefully he tested the window. It was tight. He had to wait. But within minutes, the great howling that was Dovey's prolonged series of ecstasies filled the room.

Edmund tried the window again. Three times. Four. Its stubbornness finally gave but with a slight barking moan. He waited, but Dovey's baying went unbroken. With the window open, he also heard the wild creaking of the wire spring mattress.

Using the umbrella, Edmund raised the window higher and leaned in. With outstretched arm, umbrella in hand, he tried to reach the satchel. Too far. Six inches. He got off his knees and leaned his body in farther, nearly up to his waist, careful not to snag the curtains and pull them down. The hooked handle of the umbrella stabbed at the satchel handle, repeatedly. He took a silent breath and made another waving stroke. Finally, on the next attempt, he secured the leather grip, and with great patience, began dragging it across the floor toward him.

The lovemaking never ceased.

Katie sat mortified.

Her pen lay motionless in the crook of her small hand. The strawberry flush rose into her face, and Edmund thought he'd never seen a young girl more passionately pretty. He, himself, was well past the shock of the story he had just told, but he knew Katie was only now linking up the frayed ends of this tale. The implications.

"Wait a minute," she said when her voice finally caught up to her thoughts. "Dovey killed the purple pant's man? She put the pistol under his chin?"

Katie fired through the back pages of her notes.

Edmund watched her flip the pages, letting her answer her own question.

"Here," she said. She stabbed her finger onto a paragraph written weeks earlier. "Etta's father. He was killed the same way." She looked up at Edmund then, quizzical.

"Are you up for this?" Edmund asked.

"Of course I am. You can't stop now."

Edmund gave her a serious look. "Listen here, girl. I mean it. Are you up for this? It's brutal stuff. And it doesn't get any prettier."

She stared blankly at him.

"I could go to jail, still, for the things I did." He looked away, pondering. "And you. When you know everything…you might end up hating me."

Katie shook her head. "No I won't."

"I could go to jail just for filling your head with such stuff. Abuse of a child's mind."

"Edmund, we're in this together. To the end."

Back in the trenches. From a distance, Edmund knew it was Owen—the Spartan warrior. Talking to his men. Not quite a Greek god, but striking in his dark features, abundantly loyal to his soldiers, abundantly disloyal to the war. He had lost the restful look of Craiglockhart, his face now lined with burdensome duty.

Finish this thing out, he could hear Owen saying, patting several men on the shoulders.

The tales that follow every man have twists and turns. Even in the trenches. Owen was no different, but Edmund had seen few officers who could lead better. A mother hen, clucking encouragement. *We're led by donkeys,* he said, softly, staring into their faces. *It can't be helped. Just give us your best.*

When Owen turned, he saw Lieutenant Ellicott standing there, his oilcloth-covered Krag like a third arm at his side, and he produced a bitter smile. "Are we mere ghosts now, Edmund?"

A beeline to the depot. A two-hour wait for a train heading north. Edmund's stomach was a twisting eel. Minutes dragging. The Great War seemed shorter than this, as he clung to the shadows, waiting any moment for the bearded man to reappear, looking madly for his stolen satchel. Finally, the chug and the steam and the slow dragging out of the station. Through the grimy window, caked with coal smoke, he watched the platform disappear. But Edmund did not feel safe. Not by many, many years.

On the train ride, he tried to sleep, but his mind was a random harvest of firsts. First, he had to do this, but before that first he had to do this—first. There were a thousand things, it seemed. Finally, just crossing the border of Iowa into Minnesota, his thinking leveled out, and he put together a list of steps he must take. It wasn't a game anymore. A game of following a satchel. He *had* the satchel. Now it was a game of life and death. And not just his own death.

As the sun came out of the east, Edmund tried to put events in an order he could remember. He would give himself twelve hours. And in those twelve hours, he would have to think like two people. He would have to think for himself, for Edmund Ellicott. And he would have to think for Dovey Palvone, the murderess. What would she do? What was she doing this very minute?

It was only now, with this first light of day, that Edmund carefully opened the satchel. Inside were the white bricks, the small, paper-wrapped bricks. Tearing one open he saw what he had expected all along to see—money. Lots of paper money. Laundered money, he was sure. Where it came from he had no idea. It's main source coming, no doubt, from Buffalo, but its accumulation, the origin of its amassing—in an otherwise time of national poverty—he could not guess. And he did not care.

He was not a man to understand high finance, legal or otherwise. But the Giant in Buffalo did. And so did Maxwell. And if Dovey didn't know everything, she certainly knew her part. And she had played her part to the hilt in a dark Saint Louis alley last night.

Once detrained, Edmund spoke to the ticket master at the depot window.

"Heading west. Where does this train go?"

"Seattle."

"Where else?

"Well, there's lots of places before Seattle. There's Fargo, of course. And Billings. Butte. Spokane. Wenatchee."

Edmund nodded. "Thanks."

Next, he went to the Teiko Lake ferry landing. Billy Shaw was turning a big rope, winding it into a coil on the wooden dock. When he looked up and saw Edmund approaching saw the expression on Edmund's face, Edmund's own stomach coiled, just like the rope, and Edmund knew instantly that Billy's life was about to change.

Billy listened, turning around once or twice to stare at the lake. He pulled off his cap, scratched his blond hair, and then put the cap back on. He nodded earnestly a number of times. Looking vigilantly over Edmund's shoulder in the direction of the pawnshop, he reached out his hand and received an envelope from his former teacher. Then Billy slid the white packet between the buttons of his shirt and nodded again. They shook hands and Edmund walked briskly away.

He did not find Etta in the house. Panicked, he double-checked every room. *Where?* He beat his fist on the table, tumbling the sugar bowl. He moved to the window and stared out. Down the long street, he saw the only other place she had ever gone—his classroom.

Hobbs was in a far hallway, putting a plane to a sticky doorjamb. The handyman looked up and nodded but said nothing. Edmund took the stairs two at a time, opened the door to his classroom, and took it in with one sweeping gaze. He did not see her. But turning he caught sight of her there behind the door, sitting on the floor, her knees up to her chin, her pretty dress soiled with dust from the floor. When she looked up at him, Edmund saw the bruises on her cheeks. He came to her and lifted her, held her, felt her shiver in his arms.

"He came to the house."

"Maxwell?"

She nodded.

He touched her face delicately. The bruises were plainly the tracks of Max's thumb and forefingers pinching her face. "Did he touch you anywhere else?"

"No." Her eyes fell. "But he said he would if I didn't tell."

"Tell what?"

She seemed weak now, and Edmund helped her to a chair. He allowed her to gather herself; her tears were coming now. "They...killed Bernard. He didn't..." She wiped at her face. "He found out something. Bernard did. But he wouldn't tell. Or...or else he didn't know. And they thought he did."

Edmund pulled her to him and let her weep. "And they thought Bernard told *you* something too?" he added. "Some secret?"

Through her sobs, he felt her nod against his shoulder.

"That's why you're here. That's why Wilk Palvone had me build that extra bedroom. Even before they killed Bernard. They knew they had to isolate you. Keep a close eye on you."

"And...you," she said.

Edmund realized now that he had been living in grave danger from the beginning. That marrying Dovey had been a clever scheme from the start. Appearances only. That's what the Palvones had always been about. Appearances. She could have married anyone. Jeff. Or Bently, who owned the tavern on Third Street. Or Temple Hagerty, the postmaster. It just happened to be him—stupid, horny Edmund, taken in by a woman's exotic stare. But the Palvones wanted to appear normal. Appearing normal was the first priority. And they might have pulled it off, had it not been for Uncle Victor, seeing through everything. Edmund remembered now, last winter, chopping wood together in the back of the store in Bullfork, Uncle Victor had said—*Watch out for that woman of yours.*

He held Etta away from him so he could see her face and so she could see his. "How long will it take you to pack?"

"Pack?"

"You're getting out of here. I've already made the arrangements."

"I...I don't have anything to pack. I only came with two dresses...and some underwear."

"Leave it. I don't want you going back to the house."

Edmund then told her what he wanted her to do. Right down to the finest detail.

"But what about you?"

"I'll be two days behind you."

They stood quietly, and the air around them settled at last. They heard the faint rasping of Hobbs' plane scraping at the doorjamb. Edmund put his fingers into Etta's thick hair and pressing his face close, breathed in her scent.

"Class. I want hands. Now that the shock of the ending is over, what else can you take away from this story?"

Natalie did not raise her hand. She kept her eyes on the others. Was it fear? Is that why she hesitated? Was she afraid no one would respect what she had to say?

"Mr. Worthy?"

"I thought the guy wasn't very smart. Building a fire under a tree like that."

"Okay, Worthy. What does that tell you about the man then?"

"I already said. He wasn't very smart."

"And," Mr. Ellicott continued, "what if you found out that

this particular man was a doctor. Or a lawyer."

"Or a teacher," offered Elizabeth Suttee.

"Or a teacher," Mr. Ellicott said. "Would that still make him 'not very smart'?"

The class paused, thinking.

Natalie had other thoughts to share, about the dog, but she held back.

"You have to understand, class, that the rush to the Yukon was very similar to the great gold rush of California that you learned about in history from Mr. Hooper."

A collective light seemed to pass over the class now. "Oh," said Myer Moss, anxious to be heard. "Mr. Hooper said that everybody and their uncle went west to strike it rich."

"Go on."

"So, even doctors and lawyers and…and teachers went. They all had gold fever."

"Now, considering the man's failed attempt at lighting a fire. What factors can you add to the picture?"

"Experience," said Worthy.

"No," chorused the class. "*In*-experience."

Mr. Ellicott nodded. "In his own realm, he might have been a rather clever chap. He may have even been a surgeon. Or a successful banker. But a frontiersman?"

Natalie waited. Finally, Mr. Ellicott's roving gaze fell upon her, and he knew instantly that she had more to add. He wanted her to shine. He wanted desperately to give her a nudge. He wanted to read her mind.

"There's something more though. At least in the way Mr. London has presented his tale. And it is his clever way of having certain primitive actions fly in the face of human intellect. Natalie? Do you have a suggestion?"

She fidgeted bravely. "The dog," she said. "The dog seemed… well, it seemed to have more sense than the man. I mean, at least it knew there was something wrong. And…and it knew what to do when he realized the man was frozen to death."

"Very good, Natalie. Very good."

Very good, Natalie.
Frozen to death.

Edmund let the pain settle into his chest, just above his breastbone, where everyone else resided. It was getting crowded in there. He felt like a collector of souls. He had lived too long. Collins had been there a long time. And Natalie too. Owen. Aunt Delores and Uncle Victor were there. But these last two occupied a separate place. Their lives had ended happily. They knew how to survive. Aunt Delores said it was because they had long before surrendered their lives to Jesus. *Humans think they are so blasted smart, striving as they do,* she said. *They think they've got all the answers. Ha. It makes me laugh. It probably makes God laugh.*

Suddenly, he realized that Katie was sitting there, waiting for him to say something.

It was a risk waiting until dark. Edmund half expected Dovey to arrive on the train and spoil everything. But she didn't. In fact, he supposed that she—perhaps for the first time in her life—felt utterly out of control. She had just lost the satchel. Was she still searching in St. Louis for it? Or was she on her way back to Buffalo. No. She had never gone to Buffalo. It had never been her intention. But the Giant, Wilks Palvone, would find out, sooner or later. Money was his world.

At least Etta and Billy Shaw were gone. On the train to Spokane, each with a comfortable amount of cash to see them through for a spell. Billy had bought the tickets and paid off the ticket master handsomely, instructing him to forget the whole business completely, as if it had never taken place. The ticket master had known Billy his whole life, liked him, and felt great sorrow for what happened to Natalie. The ticket master had been on the jury that convicted Hemmings. Billy watched him as he tore the transaction sheet from his logbook and put a match to it.

It would not be the only match struck that day.

Maxwell lived in the back of the pawnshop, so Edmund knew he would be there. It was the dog days of August, and the sun was slow in its decline. Earlier he had gone to the house and packed the barest of necessities. It was three weeks before the beginning of school, and what Edmund planned to do about that was the only thing that was not clear in his mind. In one bag, he packed clothes and boots. He disassembled his Krag, too, piece by piece, and after wrapping it in its oilcloth, he nestled it amongst the clothes. In the other bag, he packed his favorite books.

Uncle Victor gave a wild hoot when Edmund told him the whole story, right down to the last detail. *That crazy bitch*, he said under his breath, not wanting Delores to hear him swear. *A cold-blooded murderer, you say?* And he did not protest, even for the briefest of seconds, when Edmund placed a white-wrapped brick of money into his hands. *Delores, take the cat over to Beatrice. Tell her she can keep it. That blamed cat spends more time over there than here anyway. And pack my fiddle. We're getting on the train today.* They embraced, laughing. *As far as anybody knows, we're heading to the moon.*

The front door to the pawnshop would be locked now, Edmund knew, and the lights in the main shop area would be dark. He had brought a singletree with him, lifted from the deceased Blunt's blacksmith shop. Walking directly up to the door, he swung the heavy wooden harness brace solidly against the door, and it flew open with a jolt. Discarding the singletree, Edmund went directly to the display case and put his heel through the glass. He knew which pistol he wanted. He had seen it a hundred times.

As expected, Maxwell's footsteps came thundering across the backroom floor just as Edmund was shoving bullets into the Remington .38.

"What the hell–"

The hard metal of the Remington hit Maxwell across the temple as he emerged into the showroom, sending him to the floor. Then Edmund grabbed him by the collar and dragged him back from where he had come.

A light was on in the backroom, so Edmund scanned the room while he waited for Maxwell to shake off the blow. The wooden table, where Edmund had seen Max conduct his business, was set in neat order. The poker deck was placed in a corner of the table next to a spinning carousel of poker chips. A pile of ledgers were close by, with a pen and an inkwell. Lying beside these was a telegram, crimped at the edges, as if it had been crumpled up, folded, and then unfolded.

Edmund looked at it.

Money is gone. STOP. Stolen. STOP. What do I do? STOP.

"What did you tell her to do?"

Maxwell was rubbing his head. "What?"

Edmund picked up the telegram and waved it at Max. "Dovey. What did you tell her to do?"

Maxwell seemed confused, stunned. He clambered to his feet and collapsed in a chair. "What...are you doing?"

"I'm paying some bills," Edmund said.

"You'll die for this."

"That's how you do business, isn't it?"

Maxwell said nothing.

Edmund came behind him and kicked the chair over, tumbling Max back to the floor. This time he scrambled up quickly. He feinted a charge but stopped when he saw the pistol in Edmund's hand aimed at him.

"I have a notion to beat you to death. Calling that thug to cut out my uncle's tongue. How dare you." He stepped close and cracked Max across the nose with the pistol, causing blood to fountain into the air, thick and red.

Max fell down again. He was on his hands and knees, blood dripping onto the floor.

"And Etta. I saw the bruises."

On his feet again but keeping his distance, Max found a folded towel and held it to his nose. "I feel sorry for you, Edmund," he said, his voice muffled by the cloth. "When Dovey gets back, you're a dead man."

"You think she's coming back?"

"I know she is. That's what I told her to do."

"And she's going to kill me because I beat up her big brother?"

"She's going to kill you because she's wanted to for a long time."

"I see. A pleasure-killing?"

Maxwell laughed. "You don't know the half of it."

"I know enough. She was ten, wasn't she? I did the math. The shot under the chin. That's her trademark, isn't it?"

Maxwell appeared to flinch, eyes fluttering.

"A natural born assassin." Edmund hissed this bitterly. "She killed Etta's father, didn't she? A little girl." Edmund was so disgusted he spit on the floor. "Who would think a ten-year-old girl would have the courage…no, the sick mind, to put a pistol in a trusting Indian's chin and pull the trigger?"

This had all come to Edmund on the train ride back from St. Louis. It had been a theory, but now Maxwell confirmed it.

"She has a talent."

Edmund nodded. "I bet she made big daddy proud."

"How do you know all this?"

Now it was Edmund's turn to laugh. "Because I saw her kill Poole. In the alley. In St. Louis, you arrogant son of a bitch. I was there." He laughed again. "I have the satchel, Maxwell. I'm the one who stole it."

Max could no longer hide his shock. He swayed, as if dizzy. He looked around the room, searching for something, anything that he could use to fight back. But Edmund's pistol shot out a flash of flame and Maxwell went down hard, his kneecap blown into cinders. A familiar howling filled the room, not of pleasure though, rather of severe pain.

Edmund had never been a man comfortable with pistols. His

Krag had been an extension of his own body, another natural limb. So his hand shook as smoke seeped up from the barrel of the Remington. The shot had been loud, but the pawnshop remained dark and the people of Smithfield had long ago stopped questioning the goings-on of that peculiar establishment.

"Bernard was murdered, wasn't he?"

"Go to hell."

"You first," Edmund said, pulling back the hammer on the pistol and pressing it to Maxwell's forehead. He paused and Maxwell, his eyes pinched shut, began to plead.

"I've got questions, Maxwell. Not many, but I'd like answers."

Maxwell only groaned, holding his useless leg, blood pouring through his fingers.

"If you murdered Bernard. Or, your father did. Or, one of his henchmen. Whatever. Then, was Etta next?"

Maxwell nodded.

"And Dovey was going to do it?"

He nodded again.

"Is Dovey really coming back here?"

Maxwell shook his head. "She can't. Not...now."

"Why? Because she lost the money? Is she marked now? Is she a target?"

"More...or less," Max whimpered.

"So, Dovey is daddy's little girl. Until she screws up. Then all bets are off. Appears blood is *not* thicker than water after all. Not when it comes to daddy's money."

Maxwell said nothing, his silence confirming the truth.

Edmund had taken something else from the blacksmith shop but had left it out front. He'd needed both hands to slam the door open. But now he went back through the showroom, and out the front door, the splintered lock giving a faint, shiny glint in the reflection of the moon.

He picked up the can of kerosene and brought it back inside. He heard Maxwell moving around in the back room, but it didn't matter anymore. Reaching in through the shattered display case, he took out another pistol. An older Colt. He put a box of bullets in his jacket pocket and returned to the back room, carrying the can of kerosene.

Maxwell left a long smear of blood as he dragged himself across the floor. But he had stopped halfway to the back door, exhausted and lightheaded from loss of blood. Edmund stood over him and poured a large gulp of kerosene directly onto Max's shattered kneecap, causing him to scream and then to faint.

"Better for you that you do," Edmund said.

He poured the kerosene all around the room, leaving a soaked trail from where Max lay, then beyond into the front showroom. He threw the can down and pulled a wooden match from his pocket and lit it. The flare made him think of Mr. Purple Pant's flare, his last cigar in the alley. Then Edmund flicked the match on the trail of kerosene and watched as it made a fierce, fiery race back to Maxwell.

He left the front door hanging open to the August heat, allowing in plenty of oxygen. With only a vague memory of his mother's flaming death, he disappeared into the night.

Edmund avoided the dining hall for two days. Exhausted from the reliving of this story left him without an appetite. And without any desire for human contact. The lesson for Katie in this was for her to realize that old people are not born old. They are not like that story by Fitzgerald, about the man born backward. *Button* something. No, she had to understand that old people were young once, and that their lives were not anything like the movies. Romance was hard-fought in the old days. Danger lurked behind every tree, every dim corner. Evil villains were not limited to Grimm's fairy tales—forest goblins or cackling witches—but were real, flesh-and-blood devils out to chop a person to pieces.

Benjamin. That's it. *Benjamin Button.* He knew he'd remember if he just didn't think about it. His class had thought the whole idea a tad beyond weird. *Is this Fitz-whats-his-name off his rocker?* they wanted to know. You'll find out next year when we read *The Great Gatsby.*

Oh, I've heard of that book. Is that the same guy?

The same, Mr. Ellicott said.

"Are you sick, Edmund?" It was Brooke, poking her face through his door after supper.

"No," he answered.

She came in and stood by his chair. He was watching the ocean again and didn't want to be bothered.

"Well, we miss you. Why don't you come and do Bingo with us tonight?"

Edmund wanted terribly to tell her what she could do with her Bingo, but he was learning to mind his manners with her. The nicer he was, the more she left him alone.

"Another night maybe," he said in strained politeness. "I'm just being thoughtful. You know, being old takes up quite a bit of my time these days."

The old frame structure was an inferno within minutes, and once the ammunition heated and started going off, it put an end to all reasonable attempts by citizens to put out the blaze. No one wanted his name listed in the obituaries as someone killed by a stray bullet while trying to put out a worthless pawnshop fire. So the crowd gathered at a safe distance and watched the building dissolve into flames, and then fall to timbers, and finally into ash.

It was twenty-four hours later before a group of school-age boys, looking for treasures in the cinders, stumbled onto the charred body of Maxwell Palvone. Some believed it was an accident—a smoldering cigar. Others thought it might have been suicide. No one even suggested arson, much less murder.

Meanwhile, Edmund watched every train that entered Smithfield, even in the middle of the night. He carried the Colt in his pocket, ready, but Dovey never appeared. These were hours for deep reflection, considering all that Maxwell had confessed to. Dovey's strange behavior had risen out of the murky waters now, and she seemed to Edmund, though clearly a pathological killer, an open book.

Sitting at the depot, waiting for the 1:20 a.m. arrival, he tried to sum up every close call he might have had with her. As crazy as she was, killing him while they were having sex could very well have been a magnificent climax for her.

He shuddered.

"Tell me about Spokane." Katie was chewing gum and her breath smelled of spearmint.

"What's to tell?"

She saw him glaring past her, and she turned to see Gus sitting at a table on the other side of the activity room. "Edmund, pay attention or I'll leave."

He looked at her, scowling.

"Spokane. Tell me about it. Did you and Etta live there?"

The mention of Etta's name made him forget about Gus. "Did we?"

"That's what I asked, yes. Did you live there?"

Edmund's mind took flight, as if on a kite, and his eyes became suddenly ageless. "When I got there, I found her staying in some seedy joint by the railroad tracks. 'Etta,' I said. 'Did you see the money I gave you?' 'Yes,' she said. 'Then why are you staying in this rat hole when you could be staying uptown?' 'I was just waiting for you,' she said."

"You loved her, didn't you?"

"We moved to the Davenport Hotel. Lived in style."

"Where was Billy Shaw?"

"Left for California. He sent us a postcard."

"This is starting to sound like a fairy tale, Edmund. You know, 'happily ever after.'"

All at once, the eyes faded and his kite landed. "Not exactly," he said, his voice low, thoughtful.

"But you loved her, didn't you?"

He was seeing her again, and Katie knew it. It was as if he had quietly dismissed himself from the room, leaving his body behind. Minutes passed. Katie tried to read his mind through his eyes, but she was not old enough yet to comprehend this degree of love.

Finally he said, "Etta, Etta. *Fair and fair, and twice so fair, As fair as any may be...*"

Katie waited a while longer, closed her notebook and rose to leave, but he stopped her.

"George Peele. Ever heard of him?"

She shook her head.

"I used to read poetry to her. We'd sit by the little fountain in the Davenport lobby, and I'd read from a book. Gershwin had died by then so there were a lot of Gershwin imitators. And Cole Porter." He blinked, deep into memory. "Spokane was a happening place in those days. Etta and I taught each other how to dance. Traveling troupes passed through town. *Porgy and Bess. Anything Goes.* All the big Broadway plays were being reproduced. We never missed a show. We even met Richard Rodgers once. Etta loved that song."

Katie waited. "What song?"

"*My Funny Valentine.* She used to put on a silly showgirl face whenever it played. She'd roll her eyes up and pretend to be a star." He smiled. "She *was* a star. My star."

Edmund closed his eyes, but when he opened them, the sparkle was gone. He waved his hand across his face as if brushing at a fly, but it was the memory he wanted to push away. "Any fool could see it coming."

"See what coming?'

"She was there."

"Who was there?

"I was on the upper balcony of the Davenport. I was reading while Etta slept late. I was having a coffee. It was very early. But when I glanced down into the lobby—purely by chance—I saw her walk in. A bellboy was carrying her bag. She wore a hat. It had a long pheasant feather stuck in the band. Very stylish."

"No. Not Dovey?"

There was a prolonged hesitation.

Katie followed his face into the past.

"Etta and I talked about going to Europe. Far, far away. But Hitler was raising holy hell there. It was not a safe place. And it wouldn't be. I hope you know your history, girl. Iroquois or not. Anyone with hair as black as Etta's would have been counted among the Jews. And now Spokane wasn't safe either."

"I'm not liking where this is going," Katie said.

Edmund patted her hand. "No need to fret. She's safe now."

The movie. *The Rose Tattoo*. Saint Paul. Nineteen hundred fifty-five, the year of our Lord. Amen. He took the news clipping from his pocket. The one he'd torn from the newspaper over his late turkey dinner. He flattened it on his knee.

Death Notice.

"Breathe deep, Mr. Ellicott."

Edmund glared at the doctor. Too young to know much, he thought. "You're lucky I can breathe at all," he said. "You're getting the best I've got."

"There's a rattle in your lungs, Mr. Ellicott."

"Meaning what?"

"Meaning it sounds like pneumonia. So, we need to get that under control. I'm going to prescribe some antibiotics for you. And it's vital that you take them because–"

"Save the speech, doc. I know all about it."

"Anyway, sir. I'd like to see you in a week. See if we have it licked."

"Licked?"

The doctor smiled. "Be sure to give this prescription to the nurse at your...your–"

"At the one-foot-in-the-grave place."

There was a fever to this thing, but he didn't realize it. A temperature that started at 99.2 but then quietly, like the killer it was, crept up into the hundreds. It made the war closer. He could hear it better now. At first, it sounded like ocean waves outside his window, but he knew better. There were no oceans at the Western Front. The guns. It was the unquiet guns. The Canadian 60-pounders. The fourteen-inch railway guns. The 18-pounders. The *Mother*. It was Gershwin in gunpowder.

He followed the road where death had been the day before. A dead horse unlatched from its bracings, its once golden eye a fester of flies. Another man leading two live horses. *Lord, do what you will with this man, but spare the horses. Amen.* The soldier-dead had been moved, or buried, or laid on a bed of stacked tree branches. Wagons, broken axles, splintered wheels. A man pointing east. The Germans are over there. Beyond that canal. Waiting for us. He kept pointing.

The Tommy boys were milling. The *La Motte* farm, someone was saying, pointing east again. There they were. Company D. Manchesters. Lining the canal bank. Owen stood, handsome-headed, shoulders flexed, mothering his chicks. The steel came, a winter's blizzard of screaming bees. Into the water they plunged. But the pontoons were failing under the fuselage. *Dying, dying, God help us, we're dying.* Across, German machine guns coughed Armageddon.

In the water. Owen turned. Edmund coming behind. An

instant. Eternity. Owen's clicking fleck of cheek. *I see you.* Then back to his raft...and death, the hail too much. Things were never slow in battle. But Edmund followed the murderous spray and saw the German, the face, and the Krag buckled. The Kraut twisted—

Edmund was on his feet now. It was a miracle that he was able to get out of his bed. Slow shuffles. He was at his chair. The Krag was there, lying across the arms of the chair. It was no longer heavy in his hands. *This will be easy.* And he must do it.

Out the door. He heard the nurse's laughter. They were in the break room. The hallway was empty. Shuffle. Shuffle. The big guns were quieter out in the hall. Shuffle. The room numbers were like roosting birds above the doors.

Here. Horseface's room.

Edmund checked the Krag. *You killed Owen,* he said. How did he get inside so fast?

Gus stood before him. "*Wer ist da?*—Who goes there?"

The Krag came up.

Instinctively, Gus struck out. Edmund, teetering, missed his step and fell.

"You are...*crazy,*" Gus shouted.

"You!" Edmund tried to right himself. Failed. "You killed... you killed...you..."

"I kill *nobody.*"

Edmund tried to focus. He had been here before. He knew where to look. The bureau. The photograph. "There...there!" Still on his knees, his whole body trembled. He looked at Gus and saw Gus looking at the bureau, at the photo.

"Nooo...this is not me."

"Liar," Edmund howled. Turning his head he tried to find his Krag, but it was too far. It was across the room. No one had ever knocked his Krag from his hands before.

"No...no. Dis is not me," Gus said again.

The shaky finger then pointed to Gus' face. To his scar. "There. There. I gave that to you. I shot you. At the canal. At Sambre.

Sambre-Oise."

Gus' fingers momentarily touched the scar, and then, himself on his knees, he crawled to Edmund and pinned his arms to the floor. "Listen to me. Listen! I vas not dere. I nefer was. Look at dis eye. Look at it."

Edmund looked. "I shot you there."

"No. You could not haf. I got dis scar vhen I vas ten years old. I fell from my papa's hay vagon. I am blind in dis eye. Can't you see? I could not go to the var."

The fever came to Edmund in a wave, and he nearly fainted. Dark walls began to move around him, threatening to envelope him, shrink him, make him invisible. But it passed, and a calmness came with its passing.

"I hated the var. It...it killed my brother. There..." He pointed to the photograph. "My brother. My Gustov." And at this beloved word—Gustov—Gus broke down, his marked face a crumbled, wrecked temple of sadness. Edmund lay still. The ceiling light was like the Jesus-light, the one at the end of the long tunnel. The one he had heard so much about from the men who lay dying at his side.

"I don't usually hear the confessions of Lutherans."

"You're a priest, aren't you?" Edmund's voice was weak.

"Well, yes. I am a Catholic priest. I usually only listen–"

"Still mad at Martin Luther, are you?"

"What? No, but..."

"Listen, Father. I don't have much left in me..." He swallowed these last words. "But...but the last time I checked, God was God. This ain't India, is it? I never was in India. I hope this isn't it."

The priest smiled. "No. It's not India."

"Then listen." He lifted a weak hand and motioned. "Come close. I don't want the nurses to hear. It'll be lunchroom gossip by tomorrow."

The priest sighed.

Noting the priest's youth, he said, "What's your name, Father?"

"I am Father Marcus."

A dim twinkle. "Aren't you supposed to say, I am Father Marcus, *my son*?"

"Are you making a joke, Mr. Ellicott?"

"Only a little one."

"Very well. Mr. Ellicott, my son. Please, proceed."

"Father Marcus. I have sinned.

CONCLUSION

I kept the notes from my visits with Edmund for many years. After he died, I placed them inside a tin box. Being only a junior in high school at the time, I did not fully appreciate the treasure I possessed. I loved Edmund; of that there can be no question. He was like a porcupine who was kind enough to lay down his quills for me. Because of the life he lived, and the experiences he had in the wars, I count myself among a fortunate few whom he gave that allowance to.

Edmund went to the hospital for the last time within hours of his episode with Gus. He called it his *enlightenment*. He had knowingly discarded the prescription for antibiotics that the doctor had given him for pneumonia. So his final attack on Gus was conducted in a state of aggravated delirium. He mistook his walking cane for his much-loved Krag rifle, which, of course, altered what could have been a worse tragedy.

In the hospital, I visited him for the last time, and he told me what had happened, how he had been mistaken about Horseface from the start. It was, he said, *fueled by bitterness and loss*. He said Gus had visited him and forgave him. For me, it seemed a sad example of what might have been a fine friendship, lost through the fantasies of wartime rage.

Once I entered college and was exposed to a more thorough understanding of world events, I thought often about Edmund's experiences in The Great War, or, as he sometimes referred to it as The Great Harvest, which upon my own further study, I realize was the more appropriate name. The stories he confided in me — a too-young girl to hear such stuff, as he so often declared — were like visual monuments.

It was slaughter, and he spared me nothing. I do not think he meant any harm by it, but something in how he looked at me, something he sensed, told him that I could be trusted with the story of his life. It was a life worth guarding, and I still feel honored that it was I, on that rainy day back in 1988, who was paired with a cranky old man—a sniper, the killer of men, an arsonist, a murderer of murderers, a loyal nephew, and, above all, a great lover.

Decades have passed since then, but the flame that was Edmund Ellicott has not dimmed. It has not faded. He *was* young once, as he reminded me. And the events of his life, which I have laid down here for you, are taken directly from my notes, and from my memory of his voice. But I fear much is missing. Not from my notes, but from his own telling. He died before he could tell it all. Edmund left me with many unanswered questions.

But there are clues. And pieces of clues.

I never learned what exactly the Palvones were up to. And I'm not even sure that Edmund knew fully. Or that he cared.

Nor did he reveal just how much money was in the leather satchel. But he did tell me he never held another job, teaching or otherwise, for the rest of his life, with one exception. It was the war, the Second World War that disrupted his and Etta's life. And there was something else, too, that he did not name specifically, but that must have threatened their existence. My own conclusions centered on Dovey, and perhaps some further encounters. But it never came up.

However, the only other job was soldiering again. Although he was in his mid-40s during WWII, he enlisted with the 10th Mountain Division and fought the Germans in Italy. Through the wonders of modern technology, and through those faithful individuals who dedicate themselves to keeping official (and unofficial) records, I have found that his name appears during the heavy fighting in Torbole and shows up again as being in Trieste. He was decorated for wounds, two Purple Hearts, and for bravery.

My search for Etta was much more difficult. It took me months of searching, and it was the sole stumbling block in finalizing the telling of Edmund's story. I wanted validation. I wanted completion. But once I did find her, it became like the blooming of a flower. This led to that, and so it went. It did not answer all of my questions, but it answered some.

After Pearl Harbor, Edmund and Etta moved to Quebec. He left her there while he fought in the second war. By this time they had a child—a daughter, Rosa Delores. I next found them in Italy, after the war. They lived in Rome for a number of years. From there, their time together is lost to history.

There was one final question that evaded me. The clipping that he tore out of the newspaper while he was in St. Paul—what was it? He had found it while eating his turkey and gravy dinner on a day when he had earlier visited with an old school friend. Then he went to the theater and watched Anna Magnani in *The Rose Tattoo*. He had unfolded it there in the theater, and it read: *Death Notice*. He never told me more.

Again, with the help of computers, and with a dogged determination, I went to work tracking down old history in St. Paul. Putting everything he told me together with coinciding dates of when what theaters were showing which movies, I narrowed it down to November 16, 1955. Next came the toiling over microfiche, trying to locate newspapers from that date and the death notices that appeared in them.

My work paid off.

Death Notice: Dorothy "Dovey" Palvone of Dyer Heights, St. Paul, was found dead in her front yard yesterday. Cause of death is under investigation, but the deceased received a single bullet wound to the head. It is believed the weapon to be a high-powered rifle, fired from a distance. Palvone was a member of the Wilks Palvones of Buffalo, a prominent, well-respected family in New York.

Speculation has no place in concrete history. But I am not writing concrete history. Was this what Edmund meant when he said many times, "Etta is safe now"?

Readers, I am sure, would like to think that Edmund and Etta had many happy years together. But what finally happened to her—and to Rosa Delores—will remain unanswered, at least by me. The joy that those later years provided were kept secret to himself alone, but were revealed, nonetheless, through the tender

windows of his eyes. I asked Edmund often, in regard to Etta—
Did you love her? His answer was what lovers need never answer.
It was another of his "teacher moments," when the answer was
so obvious, the question became senseless, even stupid.

There is one photograph. It is a picture that Edmund had
hidden among his belongings and that he gave to me the day
he died. It is a black and white of Edmund, Etta, and little Rosa,
standing in front of a movie theater in Rome. They are smiling.
Edmund's arm is around Etta's shoulder and she is leaning into
him. Above them, on the marquee, the name of the Italian movie
is advertised. *The Bandit*. It is 1946. Anna Magnani is the star.

For whatever reason, I feel Rome is where Edmund and Etta
shared many of their happier moments. From that initial opening
of the bedroom door when Etta took her first steps into his life, shy
and unknowing, Edmund knew he had found his wild beauty. In
his final hours, he asked me to read to him from his favorite book
of poems. He told me he'd like to die with his old friend's words
in his ears. And so it was—

Whatever hope was yours,
Was my life also; I went hunting wild,
After the wildest beauty in the world,
Which lies not calm in eyes, or braided hair,
But mocks the steady running of the hour,
And if it grieves, grieves richlier than here...

Katharine "Katie" Marston

Acknowledgments

It is not uncommon for writers to become so involved with their characters that their sufferings and joys subsequently become real to the creator. These moments of true companionship that develop between writers and characters are some of the richest moments shared in the solitude of novelizing. Those writers who do not experience this phenomenon are to be pitied.

But aside from this, there are very real people who contribute to the development of a story. They are the technicians and those who inspire and support, without whose help the characters—indeed the very story itself—might remain adrift.

The value of intelligent offspring is that you are allowed, as a father, first rights in the areas in which they excel. Such help is inestimable. My many thanks to my son Christopher for his grasp of computer geekery; to my eldest son, Matthew, for his stoic guidance and his ability to play "father to this father" on those occasions when I needed mature application; and to my son Alex, whose love of history proved a valuable sounding board for my imagination. And thanks to my daughter Rachel (Rachel Thornton Photography) for her camera wizardry in creating my book cover.

It is a rare thing, I believe, to have an editor who not only gives generously of her time and labors in putting the polishing touches to a piece of work, but who does so with an attitude of love and respect for both the story and for the characters. Jennifer Moorman is such an editor, and my indebtedness to her is outside the limits of my vocabulary.

Many thanks to my wife, Rebecca, who has carried the bulk of this writer's scattered temperament. She stirred when stirring was needed and was calming when calming was in order. Further, from an inspirational standpoint, without Katelyn Stroud, there could never have been a Katie. And without Marla Melgoza, there could never have been an Etta.

Finally, without question, my many heartfelt thanks to the

sacrifice of poet Wilfred Owen, who through his emotionally-charged and well-crafted words, The Great War was ultimately clothed in its proper ghastly attire. It is my hope that this novel will help create a resurgence of interest in his work in classrooms everywhere.

About the Author

E. Hank Buchmann is a native of eastern Washington state where the only sea is the sea of grass from which he draws an abundance of inspiration, for both his novels and his poetry. He and his wife, Rebecca, have toured historical sites to great length, covering every corner of the United States and many glorious miles in between.

Buchmann is also the author of the *Marshal Boone Crowe* western series, which he writes under the pseudonym Buck Edwards. These titles, *Dead Woman Creek*; *Showdown in the Bear Grass*; and *Judgment at Rattlesnake Wash*, are also available through Amazon in both paperback and for the Kindle and the NOOK.

CPSIA information can be obtained
at www.ICGtesting.com
Printed in the USA
FSHW010512190421
80605FS

9 781500 478896